STO ✓

W9-BNZ-774

TOM B. AND THE JOYFUL NOISE

TOM B.
AND THE
JOYFUL
NOISE

by JEROME CUSHMAN

Illustrated by Cal Massey

THE WESTMINSTER PRESS
Philadelphia

STANDARD BOOK NO. 664–32467–3
LIBRARY OF CONGRESS CATALOG CARD NO. 70–99444

BOOK DESIGN
BY PATRICIA PENNINGTON

PUBLISHED BY THE WESTMINSTER PRESS®
PHILADELPHIA, PENNSYLVANIA

PRINTED IN THE UNITED STATES OF AMERICA

For Allan, Sandra, and the musicians

Contents

I

The Hall

Thomas Boynton Fraser, Tom B. to his friends, was swept along Bourbon Street with the noisy crowd. "Man, this is sure something," he said aloud.

It was his first visit to the French Quarter, and he could hardly believe his eyes and ears. A blaze of lights, red, green, blue, yellow, and white, flashed above the restaurants, dance halls, nightclubs, and bars. Honking cars, yelling tourists, shouting barkers, and the sound of music made a jumble of noise. Music was everywhere. It poured from almost every building. The blare of rock and roll mixed with the wail of blues and the throb of a piano, drum, and bass-fiddle combo.

Tom B.'s shoeshine box hung on his shoulder, but he was in no mood to shine shoes. There was too much going on. He felt uneasy because he had not asked his grandmother if he could come to the French Quarter. But the glitter and excitement of the street soon made him forget.

"No cover, no minimum," a barker chanted in front of a nightclub. "The show never stops. We've got the most beautiful girls in the world. It's a family show, folks, if you're over twenty-one."

The tourists who crowded the sidewalk laughed and moved on. Several stopped at a tiny art gallery, and Tom B. joined them. The walls were covered with New Orleans scenes—wrought-iron balconies, old-fashioned buildings, and paddle-wheel riverboats. An old man had set up his easel in the middle of the floor. He was trying to talk someone into having his portrait done in colored chalk.

"I'm a great artist," he bragged. "I can do a chalk drawing of anyone in thirty minutes, and it will look prettier than a photograph. I was invited by the President to do his picture, but I didn't want to make the long trip. And besides, if he wants his picture done, let him come here."

"President of what?" said one of the spectators.

The artist grinned and several people laughed.

The beat of rock-and-roll music next door drew Tom B. away from the artist. Looking inside the café, he saw people sitting at tables eating and drinking. They didn't seem to be listening to the music, even though it was so loud that they had to shout. Tom B. edged close to the door to get nearer to the band. He didn't see or hear three boys come up behind him.

"What you doing here, boy?" asked the largest boy as he waved Tom B. back to the sidewalk.

"I'm going to make me some money," answered Tom B. "What's it to you?"

"This is our corner." The second boy sounded angry.

"I don't see your name on it."

"Don't get smart," said the third.

They closed in. Suddenly, without warning, one of them lunged at Tom B. He ducked, but he caught a glancing blow on the side of his head. Someone pushed him hard, and he went down. A blaze of anger swept over him. He dropped his shoeshine box and doubled up his fists ready to fight them all. A man came to the doorway of the café.

"You all get on away from here," he said roughly. "Go on, now."

The three boys ran around the corner, giggling. Tom B., still burning, looked scornfully at the waiter, hitched his shoeshine box to his shoulder, and walked across the street.

"It ain't their street," he mumbled.

The tempting odor of meat led him to the Steak Pit, a tiny restaurant in the middle of the block. People were sitting at wooden tables. Waiters carried sizzling platters of steak. Tom B.'s stomach growled.

Better get me something to eat pretty soon, he thought.

He walked up Bourbon Street, following the crowd. Cruising cars added their headlights to the brightness around him. A sign at the corner of Bourbon and St. Peter Streets caught his eye. It read YOUR FATHER'S MUSTACHE. The waiters looked old-fashioned in their red vests, bow ties, sleeve holders, white aprons, and stiff straw hats. They served pitchers of beer and bowls of peanuts to people at little round tables.

Tom B. didn't spend much time looking through the

door of the nightclub. He stopped at the hot-dog stand parked on the sidewalk in front. He whistled. He had never seen the likes of this before. The stand was on wheels and shaped like a long hot dog. Every time the vendor reached in to get a hot dog for a customer wisps of steam escaped with a delicious smell. Tom B.'s mouth watered as he watched customers help themselves to chili sauce, ketchup, mustard, and onions. He wondered how a hot dog would taste with everything on it.

The hot-dog vendor wore a white cap perched on the back of his head. His red-and-white striped jacket and black bow tie looked sharp.

"All-meat hot dogs," he called out. "I got Mississippi dogs, Texas dogs, New York dogs, and California dogs, and they're red hot!"

"Mister, how much are the hot dogs?" Tom B. asked.

"Thirty-five cents. You want one, boy?"

"Yeah, but I ain't your boy," Tom B. said quickly, looking straight at the man. He counted his money. He had four dimes and a nickel. Business had not been good that day.

The vendor held out his hand for the money, but Tom B. didn't like the idea of paying before he was served.

"Well, do ya want it or not?" growled the vendor. Tom B. felt his anger rise, but he was hungry. He nodded and gave the man thirty-five cents.

"Watcha want on it?"

"Don't I get to put the stuff on?" he said, looking at the vendor sharply.

"Not kids," replied the vendor gruffly.

Tom B. shrugged his shoulders. "A lot of everything, please."

The vendor smiled a little and handed Tom B. a hot dog loaded and juicy with onions, mustard, ketchup, and chili sauce.

"Thank you," Tom B. said, grinning at the man. He took a large bite of the hot dog. The warm juice oozed between his fingers and ran down his chin.

"That hot dog doesn't have a chance," said the vendor as it disappeared in three or four bites. "Want another?"

"No, thanks," answered Tom B. "I'm real thirsty. Where can I get me a root beer?"

"There's a grocery store on the next corner."

Tom B. walked over to the store. With his last dime he bought a frosty cold bottle of root beer. He drank almost two thirds of it without stopping, but once his thirst was satisfied, he took ten minutes to finish the rest of the drink. Tom B. was content. He whistled happily as he walked along St. Peter Street.

A faint sound of music drew him like a magnet. People were gathered around a small window. Some were snapping their fingers and tapping their feet. Tom B. squirmed and wriggled until he worked his way to the front. Six musicians, their backs to him, were playing a drum, bass fiddle, piano, clarinet, cornet, and trombone. The music was different from any that he had ever heard. Its deep swinging rhythm was full of joy. He knew the tune, but he had never heard it played this way. It was "Just a Closer Walk with Thee." His grandmother sang it often as she worked in the kitchen, and he had sung it in church many times.

"Man, that sounds good," Tom B. said to no one in particular.

The rhythm came in restless waves. Tom B. couldn't stay still. He set his shoeshine box down. First he tapped his feet, then he shook his shoulders. In a short time his whole body was moving to the pulsing beat of the jazz music that poured out of the building. The tourists on the sidewalk made a circle around him. Dancing came easy to Tom B. His thin body moved loose and natural. The music stopped and there was a burst of clapping. Tom B. was startled and a little embarrassed, but he smiled. He wondered if his grandmother had ever heard one of her favorite hymns played like that. A man came up and put some coins in his hands.

"You're quite a dancer, kid," the tourist said, "so I asked the folks for some loose change to say thanks."

Tom B. didn't know whether to take the money or not. At least the man didn't throw it on the sidewalk the way that some grown people did.

"I wasn't asking for money," said Tom B. "I dances for the fun of it."

"That's the best way," said the tourist. He closed Tom B.'s hand on the money. "Now you buy yourself something. And keep dancing."

Tom B. counted the money. There was $1.25 in nickels and dimes. He still felt uneasy, and he wondered what his grandmother would think. He had a feeling that she would not approve of his taking the money, much less of dancing in the street for tourists.

The music started again, and he walked over to the iron gate of the musician's place. A pretty dark-haired lady sat at the entrance holding a small basket. As people went in, they dropped dollar bills into the basket. Tom B. whistled. He had never seen so many dollar bills in his life. He smiled at the lady. When she smiled back, he decided to take a chance.

"Hey."

"Hey," she replied.

"Are you the boss?" he asked.

"My husband and I are," she told him.

He glanced at the sign that hung over the wrought-iron gates. It was an unusual sign. The letters were painted on an old trombone case that hung from an iron rod.

He read aloud, "Preservation Hall."

"That's pretty good," the lady said. "Many boys your age would have a hard time with that name."

"Why you call it that?" he asked her.

"Well, you see, the musicians in there play a kind of jazz music that is famous all over the world. It's called New Orleans jazz. The musicians inside have been playing that kind of music since they were very young. Now many of them are over seventy years old. People come from France, England, Germany, Denmark, and as far away as Australia just to hear the music and meet the musicians. My," she laughed, "I made a speech."

Tom B. was impressed. He sure would like to get in and hear the musicians, but he didn't want to spend a dollar. He looked at her and grinned.

"If I tell you where you got your shoes can I get in free?"

"I'm afraid I've heard that one," she answered, "but I'll try, anyway. Is the answer, 'on my feet'?"

"Yeah," he said, a little disappointed. Then he saw the soft-drink machine in the entryway.

"You got a Coke I can buy? I'm thirsty."

"Sure, help yourself," she told him.

He was a little surprised. Although he wasn't thirsty, he walked over and put a dime in the machine. He stepped back to the gate, trying to figure out a way to get into Preservation Hall and listen to the music.

He enjoyed watching the lady greet people as they came into the Hall. She seemed to know many of them. She noticed Tom B. finishing his drink and motioned him to come inside.

"What is your name?" she asked.

"Thomas Boynton Fraser, but they call me Tom B. What's yours?"

He knew that it was not polite to ask. Grandma would put him down if she knew it. But standing boldly inside the iron gate of Preservation Hall, he waited for an answer.

"Sandra Jackson," she answered. "Where do you live?"

"At 3266 Gibson Street in the St. Bernard Housing Project. I live with my grandma, Mrs. Thomas Boynton Williams."

Sandra nodded. "Does your grandmother know you are in the French Quarter this late at night?"

Tom B. did not answer. Instead, he changed the subject.

"How much do it cost to listen to the music?"

"Is this the first time you have been here?" she inquired.

"Yes, ma'am."

"We have a special price for newcomers like yourself," she said. "Is a dime O.K.?"

"Yes, ma'am," he answered heartily, scarcely believing his good luck.

"Have a good time," she said, as he tossed a dime into the basket.

Tom B. walked into a shabby room crowded with people. Some sat on the floor. Others were on benches and old chairs. There were no seats for most of the audience, and people stood in the back of the room. Tom B. sat down right in front of the man who played trumpet. He had never heard such music. Feet tapped, hands clapped, and bodies swayed to its joyful sound. The clarinetist sang a song called "Didn't He Ramble" and the audience clapped, stamped, whistled, and shouted. Tom B. had never felt such joy in his life.

The instruments in the band were trombone, trumpet, clarinet, banjo, piano, drums, and bass viol. Tom B. liked the trumpet best. It always announced the next number by sounding a few bars of the tune. It seemed to lead the other instruments. Tom B. could not stay still long. Soon he was tapping his feet and clapping his hands in time with the music. The players grinned and pointed to him. The leader watched Tom B. and nodded his head. He was a heavyset man with gray wavy hair. His short pudgy fingers made the trumpet growl, wail, and cry out in blasts of rhythm and sound that made Preservation Hall crackle with excitement. Everyone was having a good time.

A man came into the room carrying a phonograph record. He introduced each musician by name and the audience applauded each in turn.

Then he said, "There is music here every night from eight thirty to twelve thirty. We have some fine recordings of the musicians you have been listening to. They are for sale by the gate."

When he finished, the musicians left their chairs and went into the hallway. Many of the people from the audience went out to talk to them. Tom B. looked around the room. Paintings covered the walls, and every painting was a portrait of a musician. One painting held his eyes. It showed a stocky man holding a horn in his left hand. He wore a cap with the words "Eureka Brass Band" on the rim. A small bag was slung across his shoulder. Tom B. had seen that face somewhere before. Then Tom B. recognized the musician. He was so excited that he walked over to Sandra at the front gate.

A pleasant-looking fellow stood beside her. Before Tom B. could open his mouth, Sandra said, "Tom B., this is my husband Allan."

"Hi," Allan said.

"Hey," Tom B. answered. He was too excited to be more than barely polite. "Miss Sandra, that picture on the wall—is it the man playing the horn in there?"

Some people came into the Hall and Sandra was busy, but Allan answered, "That's right. It is Willie Lewis, leader of the Eureka Brass Band."

"What's he got in that little sack on his shoulder?"

Allan chuckled. "That little sack is for music."

Willie Lewis himself was sitting on a bench in the entry hallway.

"Here's the young foot tapper," he told the other musicians. "Come on over here, young man, and let me see you."

Tom B. felt shy and a little frightened. He walked over to Willie Lewis.

"What's your name, young man?"

"Thomas Boynton Fraser, sir," he replied.

"That's quite a name for a boy your size. Think you can grow into it?" asked the musician with a grin.

"It was my grandfather's name," answered Tom B. quietly.

"Well, my name is Willie Lewis. How do you do?"

"Fine," said Tom B.

"How do you like the music?" the trombonist asked.

"Fine, but I really like that horn," he said without thinking.

"What horn? I play a horn," said the trombonist, pretending to be angry.

"His," said Tom B., and he pointed to Willie Lewis.

"How come you don't like the trombone?" the trombonist said severely. The men laughed.

Tom B. was puzzled. For a few seconds he didn't know what to say. Then he saw that the trombonist wasn't really angry.

"I like every one of you all. I ain't never heard such music before. When I hear the music I feel like dancing all the time."

He ran out of words to tell how deeply he felt about the music.

"You're all right, kid," said the drummer.

"Want a Coke?" asked the pianist.

"No, thank you, sir."

Tom B. sat in a dream world of happiness as the musicians talked together. He felt comfortable among the voices speaking of music. At home there was only grandmother. He didn't often get a chance to hear men talk.

Mr. Willie Lewis, he's the greatest, thought Tom B. to himself.

"Jim, don't forget the parade Saturday," Willie Lewis said to the trombonist. "It starts at ten o'clock from the Tulane Aid and Pleasure Club."

"I'll be there," answered Jim, "and I'll have my walking shoes on."

"We had all better have on our walking shoes, because the parade lasts until five o'clock," laughed Willie.

Allan came up and said, "It's time to start."

"Right," Willie answered, and he walked into the room, followed by the members of the band. Soon "Fidgety Feet," an old-time jazz tune, set the audience to hand-clapping and foot-tapping.

"What do Mr. Lewis mean when he say 'parade'?" Tom B. asked Sandra.

Sandra looked at him with surprise. "Do you mean that you've never seen a parade?"

"Sure I have. I been to all kinds of Mardi Gras parades,

but I never heard of a parade at the Tulane Aid and Pleasure Club. What's that?"

"You see," Sandra told him, "the musicians are hired by a club, and they play music and march in the streets. They do this once a year. Everybody is welcome to come along and follow the musicians."

"You mean, could I come?"

"Of course," replied Sandra. But she added, "The club members like to march in the street. The rest of us follow the parade from the sidewalks. We are called the Second Line."

"Do a lot of people come?" Tom B. asked, his eyes shining.

"Sometimes a thousand people follow a parade through the streets. Why don't you come Saturday if it is all right with your grandmother? Allan and I will be there."

"Where is it?" he asked.

"At Gravier and South Roman Streets, behind St. Joseph's Church. It's uptown. Anyone can tell you how to get there."

Tom B. made up his mind quickly. "You can look for me at the parade. I'll be there."

Sandra looked at her watch. She put her hand on his shoulder and said kindly, "Tom B., I really think you should go home now. It's late and your grandmother will be worried. Besides, tomorrow is a school day."

He did not want to leave. He lingered at the door, looking at her to see if she might let him stay longer, but her eyes told him that he would have to leave. Slowly he hitched his shoeshine box to his shoulder.

"Can I say good-by to Mr. Lewis?" he asked.

"Certainly."

He went into the room. Willie Lewis was playing a solo. Tom B. listened until the number was finished. He walked over to the musician.

"I've got to go now," he said.

"Good night, Tom B.," said Willie, and he shook Tom B.'s hand.

"Good night, Tom B.," said Sandra as he walked past the iron gates of Preservation Hall.

He smiled weakly. "Good night," he said.

Bourbon Street was a humming beehive. The sidewalks were so crowded that it was hard to walk without being jostled. The street was a loud jumble of auto horns, shouting people, and raucous music. Tom B. no longer cared about the sights of the French Quarter. His mind was overflowing with Preservation Hall. He imagined himself in a jazz band playing a shining trumpet like Willie and enjoying the applause of the audience. He stepped off the curb. A blast from an automobile horn shattered his dream and made him jump a mile.

"Watch out where you're going! Want to get killed?" shouted an angry voice.

Tom B. made his way through the crowd until he reached Canal and Basin Streets, where he caught the bus for home.

2

The Sinful Noise

Tom B. heard the alarm clock in his grandmother's bedroom. But he did not want to get up. It was snug and warm in his bed, and he could feel himself slowly drift back into sleep.

His grandmother's voice made him awake with a jump. "Tom B., get out of the bed right now. You hear?"

He put his head under the covers so that her voice sounded far away. He didn't hear the bedroom door open, but when he peeked out from under the covers, there she was, standing by the bed, a large spoon in her hand.

She shook it at Tom B., and her voice sounded angry. "Get up, boy, or I'll crack you with this oatmeal spoon." He noticed her grin as she waved the spoon in the air.

"Coming, Mom," Tom B. answered, hopping out of bed. He had called his grandmother "Mom" ever since the day she had told him his mother would not be back to live with them.

Lulamae Williams was a small woman, thin and wiry. Her walk was quick, and she did everything in a hurry. She always wore a simple cross on a chain around her neck. A gray hairnet matched her hair. Though she looked her sixty years, she was strong and active. She worked as a cook in a home by Lake Ponchatrain. Every morning she left for work before Tom B. went to school, and she did not get home until after seven o'clock in the evening. Sometimes it was later.

After Tom B. washed and dressed, he went into the kitchen. It was his favorite room in the house. Everything in it was clean and bright. The walls were painted eggshell white and an African violet in full bloom was gay against the white window curtain.

This morning Tom B. could see that something was troubling his grandmother as she filled his dish with hot oatmeal. He poured milk and sprinkled brown sugar on the oatmeal and waited for her to speak. He knew that she would, sooner or later.

"Thomas Boynton Fraser," she said in a tired voice, "what time did you get home last night?"

He had made it a point not to look at the clock when he got home. "I don't know, Mom, honest I don't."

"Well, I know one thing. It was after twelve o'clock. I couldn't stay up and wait for you any longer. I got to get my rest, you know that. I work hard all day."

Tom B. had expected her to be angry and maybe yell at him. He didn't know what to say when she was sad. She looked old and tired. Tears started in the corner of his eyes. He felt guilty.

"I know you want to make a little spending money for yourself shining shoes downtown, but I want you home early," she went on. "It isn't good to be out alone at night and me not knowing where you are."

"Mom, I won't go downtown tonight," he said in a quiet voice, his lips quivering. "And the table will be set when you come home," he added, trying to make up for the unhappiness he caused her.

She didn't answer, but sighed and got ready to leave for work. "Don't forget your lunch, and study hard in school today, you hear? I want you to be somebody when you grow up. Without schooling you're nobody."

"Yes, ma'am," he answered and felt good again. He knew that he was forgiven.

"Hush that 'Yes, ma'am' unless you mean it," she said severely. "Your teacher tells me you're a good scholar when you want to be, but you're a dreamer. Keep your eyes open, boy, and learn something. Pass by here and kiss me good-by."

"Good-by, Mom," he said as he kissed her.

"I want to see your face when I come home tonight."

"My face will be here, and so will the rest of me," he laughed.

His grandmother's stern look melted into a grin and he heard her say to herself as she walked out of the door, "That boy, he's just like his grandfather, God bless them both."

Tom B. went to his room to make the bed. He liked his room with its ladderback chair, dresser, and bunk bed. The walls were decorated with old Mardi Gras posters and a faded Tulane University pennant. His ball, glove, and bat were in the corner.

"I almost forgot," he said to himself. "I'd better put away my loot." He opened the dresser drawer and took out a small cardboard box. "Man," he exclaimed hap-

pily, "I've got me almost twenty-five dollars." A plan
was forming in his mind. It had something to do with
Willie Lewis, Preservation Hall, and jazz music.

He went into the kitchen and saw the lunch that his
grandmother had fixed—peanut-butter-and-jelly sandwich, banana, and a candy bar. There was a nickel for
milk money too.

"Mom always remembers my milk money," he
chuckled. Whistling "Didn't He Ramble," he left for
school.

A new school had just been finished in the neighborhood. It was a welcome change from the old army bar-
racks that had been his school last year. He liked the
bright brick-and-steel building. The schoolroom was
cheerful, with plenty of space for chairs and desks. He
remembered how uncomfortable he had been at his old
desk that was nailed to the floor. The green blackboard
and yellow chalk were fun to use.

Tom B. liked school, especially arithmetic. He could
look at a problem and often come up with the answer
without using pencil and paper. This pleased his grandmother and his teacher, Miss Garland. She was a good
teacher and he liked her, but she seemed to pay more
attention to him than to many of the other students. This
bothered Tom B. He didn't want to be called teacher's
pet. He did like it, though, being praised when Miss
Garland told him he did good work.

Geography class was dull. Usually, working with maps
and finding out about people all over the world was exciting, but not today. Tom B.'s mind wandered to Preservation Hall and the music of Willie Lewis and the

band. He had never heard music played so beautifully. He remembered how Willie held the trumpet and how it seemed alive in his hands. He remembered the joy of the audience, their hand-clapping and foot-tapping. Soon he was in the middle of a sound-and-color daydream. He was in front of a jazz band, playing the trumpet with ease and beauty. The sweet sound of applause rang in his ears. The applause was silenced by the splat of a ruler on the teacher's desk.

"Tom B., I've asked you twice," said Miss Garland. "What states are bounded by Louisiana?"

Tom B. jumped in his seat. Without thinking he blurted out, "Preservation Hall."

The class exploded with laughter. Miss Garland smiled. "I don't think so. They tell me that it is bounded by Bourbon, St. Peter, and Royal Streets in the French Quarter."

Tom B. was embarrassed. "Could I have the question again, please?"

Miss Garland, her patience getting shorter, repeated it. Tom B. answered quickly, "Texas, Arkansas, Mississippi, and the Gulf of Mexico, which isn't a state." He grinned.

"Correct," she replied, pleased with her student, "but I wonder how Preservation Hall crept into our geography lesson?"

During arithmetic Tom B. was called upon to go to the blackboard and do problems. He made simple mistakes in addition. He did not seem to have the slightest idea how to work problems that he usually found easy.

It was no use. Snatches of old jazz tunes that he had

heard the night before ran through his mind. He started humming to himself, keeping time on top of his desk with his fingers. He heard giggling, and he looked around. Everyone was looking at him. Miss Garland was trying not to smile, and his classmates put their hands over their mouths, but giggling noises sounded all over the room.

"Tom B., it seems as if today is your day for music. I don't know what has come over you," said the teacher.

"I'm just not with it, I guess." He tried to figure how angry she was.

"You certainly are not," she replied. "I hope that you'll straighten out over the weekend. I hope you'll come back to school on Monday ready to pay attention to what is going on around here."

School was a drag for the rest of the day. He didn't care whether Miss Garland caught him daydreaming or not. He had important things to think about, like the parade on Saturday. What would it be like? Would Willie Lewis talk with him? Would he see Sandra and Allan? The word "parade" flashed through his mind.

"That's it," he said to himself. "I'll have a parade of my own after school."

At last the bell rang and the children flocked out into the street. Tom B. ran the few blocks to his apartment. He went inside and put his books on a little shelf in his bedroom. Several of his friends were waiting when he came outside.

"Come on, Tom B.," Tim called, "let's play ball."

"I don't want to play ball today," answered Tom B.

"Why not?"

" 'Cause I got another game that's more fun." Tom B. looked mysterious.

"What game you got?" asked Bill.

"Jazz parade," Tom B. announced.

"How you play this game?"

"Just you go get anything that will make music and carry it here. We'll have us a real New Orleans parade," he answered.

Tom B. dug into his closet and brought out an old battered toy trumpet that someone had given him when he was four or five years old. He looked at it, frowning.

"Kid stuff," he said, "but it's the best I got."

The boys came back with an odd collection. There were tambourines, combs covered with tissue paper,

washboards, harmonicas, and assorted pots and pans.

"Line up," Tom B. ordered. The boys dutifully lined up behind him. "Ready, go," he shouted.

A blast of noise startled the neighborhood. The parade moved slowly in a scraggly line with Tom B. marching proud in front. Smaller children playing nearby ran to see what was going on. They joined the parade, laughing and shouting. The line marched across the street, past the ice-cream store, the Texaco filling station, and the school. Tom B. wasn't leading a pretend parade in the St. Bernard Housing Project. He was leading the Eureka Brass Band. The deafening noise made by the odd instruments was really the rolling rhythm of "The St. Louis Blues," just as he had heard it at Preservation Hall.

The parade moved happily along. More children joined, and more, until it seemed as if every young child in the housing project was marching. The noise grew louder and louder. The marchers circled around the school and back to the housing project, tramping in and out of the courtyards. Mothers, grandmothers, older brothers and sisters came outside to watch. They shouted and clapped their hands in the spirit of the good time.

Tom B. led the parade to the front of his home. He raised his arm for the noise to stop. The noise was still in a few seconds.

"I got to go in and set the table for supper," announced Tom B.

The others tried to get the parade started again, but

without Tom B. everyone lost interest. One by one they
wandered off. In five minutes no one was left.

He took a hot bath, because he knew that his grandmother would ask. Then he set the table. He decided to
work a few arithmetic problems. For the fun of it he
went to the part of the book that Miss Garland had not
explained. He worked on arithmetic until he heard his
grandmother's footsteps.

"Hey, Mom," he said cheerfully as he opened the door.
"You're home early tonight."

"Hello, boy," answered his grandmother. "Have you
had your bath?"

"Yes, ma'am," he chuckled.

"I see the table is set. Well, it looks like you've been a

good boy today. Pass by here and give your grandma a kiss."

Tom B. kissed her and grinned happily. He was full of things to tell her.

"Mom, I worked out some problems that Miss Garland hasn't showed us how to do."

"You've got a head on you for figures, just like your grandpa," she smiled at him. "Did you do good in school today?"

"Good enough, I guess," he answered. He went on excitedly, "Mom, last night I found a place in the Quarter called Preservation Hall. I heard the Willie Lewis Band play. It was great."

The words poured out. He told her about Preservation Hall and the music and how much he liked it. He was so eager to tell her everything about his adventures that he didn't notice the deep frown on her face.

"And today after school we played jazz band. I was the leader."

Suddenly he saw that she was angry, angrier than ever before. But it was too late to take his words back.

"So that's where you were last night. Jazz band. So you played jazz band." Her voice was shrill. It rose higher as she grew angrier and angrier. She fixed her blazing eyes on him and he felt smaller and smaller. "You know I don't allow no jazz music in my house," she went on. "That's sinful music. Preservation Hall, indeed. I don't ever want you to have anything to do with those men. They are trashy people."

Tom B. had a funny feeling in his stomach and a lump

in his throat. He was hurt by her terrible anger and crushed, but he tried to explain.

"Mom, I talked with some of the musicians, and they is nice. Willie Lewis is famous all over the world, and the folks who run the place was good to me, and—"

She stopped him with a stamp of her foot. "Thomas Boynton Fraser, hear me! I've been saved by the Lord, and my church tells me that you can't love the Lord and the devil's music at the same time. I won't allow you to have no truck with jazz music."

"But, Mom," began Tom B. His voice broke into a sob.

"That's all. I don't want to hear no more."

Tom B. swallowed hard. His half-formed plan to buy a trumpet, to learn music, or even to see Willie Lewis again melted away.

Supper was dreary. Instead of chatting back and forth, both were too troubled to speak. They ate in silence and did not look at each other.

Right after supper Tom B. excused himself and went to his room. He got into his pajamas and turned out the light. Sleep did not come for a long time. The more he thought about his grandmother's anger, the more hurt he became. He lay in bed and tried to sort out his feelings.

"Why did she turn on me like that? I didn't do anythink wrong," he fumed to himself.

He thought about the parade at the Tulane Aid and Pleasure Club tomorrow. The angry voice of his grandmother came to him. *I won't allow you to have no truck with jazz music.*

Should he go?

3 1526656

The Parade

Usually Tom B. slept until nine or ten o'clock on Saturdays, but today he woke up at seven thirty. His grandmother bustled about the kitchen. When he came into the room, she didn't say anything. He looked at her.

"Good morning, Mom," he said quietly.

"Good morning," she answered curtly. "You're up mighty early today."

"Couldn't sleep no more." He added quickly, "I thought I'd get up and help you a little. Want me to take the clothes over to the laundromat?"

"It would help out a lot," she said. "Wash up first and eat your breakfast."

After breakfast Tom B. put the basket of clothes in his wagon and went to the laundromat two blocks away. He waited by the churning machines, and thought about the parade uptown. What harm could hearing some music do? The more he thought about the parade, the sorrier he was that he had sort of tried to make up with his grandmother.

"Grandmothers sure are old-fashioned," he muttered. "It ain't fair."

He made up his mind. "I'm going to that parade, no matter what," he said to himself.

His grandmother was waiting for him, and he helped her fold the clothes.

"I suppose you're going downtown to shine shoes to-day," she said.

He nodded yes, hoping that she wouldn't ask any more questions.

"I want you to stay away from those docks. Henry Sancton told me he saw you there one day last week."

"I won't go to the docks, Mom," he promised. But he thought, so that's how she found out I go to the docks—from Henry Sancton!

"The docks are dangerous with all that ship-loading. Henry told me that a box came loose and fell on a man loafing around the place. That man woke up in Charity Hospital, and he won't walk for a long time. You stay away from there," she finished sharply.

"Yes, ma'am," he answered. He was sorry that he had to promise her. It was fun at the docks, watching the cranes lift huge loads onto the ships. There was always something going on at the docks. He loved to watch the ships come and go on the Mississippi River.

He went to his room to get his shoeshine box. He took along a dollar's worth of nickels and dimes, just in case he needed change.

"I'll be going now, Mom."

"You be back before dark," his grandmother called after him.

She did not kiss him good-by, and he had an empty

feeling in his stomach. As he walked to the bus stop, he tried to whistle cheerfully. It was a sorry sound.

He got off the bus in front of the Krauss Company Department Store and walked down Canal Street toward the French Quarter. He didn't want to take a chance on being late to the parade, so he asked the way from a man selling papers on the corner.

"I need to go to Gravier and South Roman Street, please, sir," he asked.

The man pointed and said, "Go over to Tulane Street and go up Tulane to the bus station. You'll find your street behind the bus station."

When Tom B. reached the bus station, he got an idea. Why not put my shoeshine box in a locker to keep safe while I go to the parade? He found the Tulane Aid and Pleasure Club easily, because there was a crowd of people gathered in front. The club was a small two-story building. Members were going in and out of the club, and Tom B. noticed that the men were smiling and joking. He felt that a celebration was going to happen, something like a big party.

He saw the musicians standing together by the steps. Some of the men he remembered from Preservation Hall, but there were many he did not know. He saw Willie Lewis.

"Hey, Mr. Lewis," he shouted.

"Well, here you are, just like you said," Willie greeted him.

"Is this your band, too, Mr. Lewis?" Tom B. asked.

"Not exactly. You see, the men elected me leader. If I

don't do well, they might elect someone else to take my place." He laughed.

"The Eureka Brass Band." Tom B. read the labels on the caps the musicians wore.

"Sure is," said Willie.

"Does the band play at Preservation Hall?"

"Not very often," Willie answered. "You see, we're a marching band. We play for parades, churches, store openings, big affairs like that."

"Man, it's a big band." Tom B. counted the men. There were three playing trombone, two on trumpet, one cornet, a saxophone, a clarinet, a tuba, a bass drum, and a snare drum.

Willie chuckled. "Oh, yeah. We can make a lot of noise if we want to. I've got some business to tend to. The parade will start pretty soon. I'll see you."

Tom B. felt the excitement of the crowd as the time for the parade drew near. About two hundred people were waiting for the music. Children ran here and there. Camera bugs were busy snapping pictures of the musicians and club members.

Someone shouted, "Here comes the Queen." A white convertible drove up. It was decorated with wax flowers of red, green, blue, yellow, and white. Tom B. caught his breath. The Queen was a beautiful young lady. She wore a long white dress covered with sequins that glittered in the sunlight. A red velvet cape trimmed with white fur was draped around her shoulders. She wore a jeweled crown and carried a scepter that sparkled like diamonds. She smiled and talked with the people who pressed close to her car to see her.

The band tuned up with a delicious collection of sounds. Tom B. could feel a buzz of excitement flow through the crowd. The band lined up in the middle of the street, and one by one the club members lined up behind it. One man carried a large American flag and another carried a blue-and-gold banner that said "Tulane Aid and Pleasure Club, Organized 1904." The club members were dressed alike, tan hats, shirts, and trousers, white suspenders, and brown-and-white shoes. Several carried baskets full of bright wax flowers.

Willie Lewis blew a few notes on the trumpet. The crowd grew tense at his signal for the music to begin. The snare drum rattled. The bass drum boomed three times. With a rhythmic roar the Eureka Brass Band made music for a New Orleans parade.

The crowd cheered and moved with the band. The members of the Tulane Aid and Pleasure Club marched. The younger members danced to the rhythm of jazz music played in four-four time.

Two men marched in front of the band. One was a large jolly-faced man who wore a black derby hat, a long-tailed coat, and a red sash draped across his shoulders with the words "Eureka Brass Band" in large shiny letters. He carried a large fan of red feathers with the letter "E" on the front and back. He marched with a proud step and easy grace. Children did their best to copy his strut.

His partner was a small white-haired man. He also wore a black derby and a long-tailed coat. His sash was black against the white front of his shirt. He had a pipe in his mouth and carried a red umbrella decorated with

colored tassels. His march step was a slow dance shuffle
called a Slow Drag. So many photographers wanted
to take their picture that the two men had a hard time
getting through the crowds.

"Who are they?" Tom B. asked one of the bystanders.

"The big one is Fats Houston and the little one is Slow
Drag Pavegeau," he answered. "They are the Grand
Marshals of the Eureka Brass Band."

Tom B. was filled with excitement. He danced as he
had never danced before. His shoulders shook, his hips
swayed, and his feet flew like sparks on the pavement.
He laughed with sheer joy.

Children ran far ahead of the band, dancing, marching, and shouting. People crowded the windows and
balconies of the houses as the parade passed. They
waved to friends who were following the parade. They
waved to the musicians. More and more people joined
the parade as it slowly moved along the street.

The band played three numbers, and then it rested.
But the march went on to the beat of the snare drum.
Tom B. walked beside Willie Lewis.

"Can I carry your horn for you?" he asked.

"Certainly," said Willie, handing the trumpet to him.

Tom B. noticed a group of men and boys who seemed
to stay together. One of them carried a sign with the
words, "Sixth Ward Second Liners."

"Who are them people?" Tom B. asked Willie.

"They have been following parades for years," Willie
said. "When they hear about a parade, they call each
other and meet so they can march together. They are a

sort of club too, but they can't afford to pay for a band of their own."

"Miss Sandra said she was a Second Liner."

"That's right. Everyone is a Second Liner except the organization that pays for the music."

The music started again. Tom B. was marching beside Willie Lewis when he felt a hand on his shoulder. He turned and saw Allan and Sandra. Sandra took one of his hands and Allan the other, and the three of them marched to the music. The band stopped in front of a frame house, and the musicians and club members went inside.

"What are they doing?" Tom B. asked.

Allan said, "They are stopping for sandwiches and coffee or cool drinks. After they rest for a few minutes, the parade will start again. By the way," he asked, "are you thirsty?"

"My mouth feels like a cotton patch," grinned Tom B. They went to a filling station, and Allan bought Cokes for all. Tom B. finished his in a few gulps.

"Want another?" Allan asked.

"Yes, please," replied Tom B.

He drank another Coke and his mouth felt better. "Do you go to all the parades?" he asked.

"Not all," Sandra laughed, "but quite a few. We can't stay long today because we have some work to do at the Hall."

"Can I have a job at the Hall?" Tom B. suddenly asked Allan.

"I'm afraid not. You see, we are open at night, and

children aren't allowed to work past seven o'clock."

"How about after school?"

"Your grandmother probably needs you then," Allan said. "But we'll think about it," he added.

The musicians came out of the house, and soon the parade got under way. By this time the crowd was so large that the streets and sidewalks were covered with people. Tom B. lost Sandra and Allan, so he made his way back to Willie Lewis.

The sun was hot, and sweat ran down into his eyes. He saw that some of the musicians tied white handkerchiefs around their necks. He did the same. The parade didn't seem to follow any particular route, but turned up this street, down another, and wound around neighborhoods where there were housing projects and many people.

Tom B. was tired and his feet hurt, but he kept going. Some of the streets looked familiar to him. The band rounded a corner. Why, they were within a block of the Tulane Aid and Pleasure Club! The parade would end where it began. Tom B. could hardly see the band through the huge crowd of people. But he could hear them play two more numbers, "Joe Avery's Tune" and "Take Your Burden to the Lord." Suddenly the parade was over. The crowd melted away quickly.

Tom B. went up to Willie Lewis. "Thank you for the music, Mr. Lewis. I really liked it," he said shyly.

"You're mighty welcome, Tom B.," answered Willie. He paused for a minute, then he asked, "Have you eaten?"

"No, sir."

"Do you think it would be all right with your folks if you went home with me and had a bite?"

"Just so I get home before dark," Tom B. answered.

"It will cheer up my wife to have a boy to feed. We've got a grandchild your age, but we haven't seen him for a long time. My car is around the corner. Let's go."

4

The Lesson

Tom B. said very little in the car. He tried to keep his eyes from drooping, but it was hard to keep them open. Once he sat up with a start. He had almost fallen asleep.

"What's the matter, Tom B., you tired?" Willie asked.

"No, sir, I'm not tired," answered Tom B., but his head kept nodding. The next thing he knew, he was awakened when the car stopped. He sat up quickly.

"I believe you had a little nap," chuckled Willie.

"I wasn't asleep. I was only resting," said Tom B.

He liked Willie's house. It was white with gray trim. A crepe myrtle tree, a hibiscus bush, and three different kinds of roses grew in the tiny front yard. There was an old-fashioned swing on the front porch.

"Hungry?" Willie asked.

"Sure am," answered Tom B.

"I'm sure Mrs. Lewis will have a little something for us to eat," Willie said, "but it might not be fancy food."

"It don't make me no mind. I'll eat what's set before me. Mom taught me that."

"Your mother taught you well."

"Mom is my grandmother," Tom B. said in a low voice. Willie didn't answer.

"Can I swing, Mr. Lewis?"

"Let's go in and meet the missus first."

They went into a neat living room. Tom B. saw the piano in the corner. On top of it was another trumpet case, older than the one that Willie brought from the parade. A photograph of a man, a woman, and two children sat on the living-room table.

A large woman with a pleasant smile came into the room. Willie greeted her with a kiss.

"This is Thomas Boynton Fraser," he introduced Tom B., "and he likes jazz music and parades. Tom B., meet Mrs. Lewis."

"How do you do," said Mrs. Lewis. She shook Tom B.'s hand.

"Fine, thank you, ma'am," he answered.

"Do you play an instrument?" she asked.

"No, ma'am, but I'd sure like to," he replied.

"What would you like to play?"

"A horn like Mr. Lewis," he said quickly.

Willie and his wife laughed. She looked at her husband and said, "Remember when you used to sneak under his window and listen to Peter Bocage practice. You'd sneak away from home and take the ferry across the river to Algiers and be gone all day."

"I remember what happened to me when I got home too," said Willie. "Man, did I get spanked."

"I suppose you men are hungry," said Mrs. Lewis.

"Yes, indeed," answered Willie. He turned to Tom B. "I'll tell you what, supposing you have a little ride on the porch swing. I'll call you when we're ready."

Tom B. needed no further urging. A porch swing was something new in his life, and he enjoyed the feel of moving back and forth in happy rhythm.

A few minutes later Willie called, "Tom B., you want to come in and wash up? We'll be ready to eat in a minute or so." He went inside.

"Come and get it," Mrs. Lewis called. "Sit here between us so we can both talk to you," she said to Tom B.

When they sat down, Willie and Mrs. Lewis bowed their heads. Tom B. was surprised, but he hurriedly copied them and was astonished to hear the same grace that his grandmother said before meals. This puzzled him, but he was too hungry to think about it. His plate was filled to overflowing with spare ribs, green beans, mashed potatoes, and lettuce salad, and Mrs. Lewis put a tall glass of milk by his plate. He ate hungrily.

"My, you're quite an eater," said Mrs. Lewis. "I like to see boys eat well. I remember when our boy was small, it seemed to me that he ate as much as his daddy."

"How old is your boy?" Tom B. asked.

"He's a man now, thirty-one years old," Willie answered. "He's married and lives in Los Angeles, where he's a foreman in a plant. We've got two grandchildren."

"Did he go to college?" Tom asked.

"Oh, yes," Mrs. Lewis said, "but there wasn't work for him here when he graduated, so he went out to California."

Tom B. ate until he was comfortably full. Mrs. Lewis went to the refrigerator and came back carrying a large pecan pie. "A piece of pie and another glass of milk is just the thing to finish your meal. O.K.?"

"O.K.," answered Tom B. "Man, just look at that pretty pie."

"Now, that's what I call appreciation," laughed Mrs. Lewis. She cut him a big slice.

"Do you go to church, Tom B.?" asked Mrs. Lewis.

"Sure do, ma'am. Mom and I go to church every Sunday. She is a deaconess," he added proudly.

"That's good," Mrs. Lewis said. "We're churchgoing people too. Willie is a deacon in the Gloryland Baptist Church."

Now Tom B. knew why they had said grace at the table, but he still didn't understand. "You mean you go to church and play jazz music too. How come?"

Willie and his wife laughed heartily. "Of course," Willie said. "What's wrong with jazz music? I thought you liked it."

Tom B. was mixed up. "I do, but Mom says to play jazz music is sinful and that jazz musicians . . ." He caught himself just in time from saying "trashy."

A look of pain and anger crossed Willie's face. He looked at Tom B. a moment, his eyes flashing. Then he said slowly, "My own mother and father believed the same way as your grandmother. But when I learned music, I naturally learned how to play all kinds of music. One Sunday I was playing 'Just a Closer Walk with Thee' in church. I played it sad-like and people cried, my mother and father too. I didn't like to see them crying, so I started playing it jazz style. Everyone perked up and started clapping their hands. After that it was all right with my parents for me to play jazz music. Tears and joy both come from God," he added firmly.

"Mom doesn't allow jazz music in her house," Tom B. said.

"That's too bad," Willie answered. "Jazz music makes people feel good. It is happy music. People have a right to be happy, and jazz music helps. It's sad music too. We tell each other our troubles with music. Sometimes we have to be sad. A man can't be happy all of the time. Seems like our people have a hard time snatching a little happiness from all the sorrow that we share. But most important, jazz music comes from the heart. It's honest. That's why people come from all over the world to hear jazz music in New Orleans."

Tom B. decided to have a talk with his grandmother. He wished she could meet Willie and Mrs. Lewis. His misery about liking jazz music fell away. But he remembered that he had disobeyed his grandmother, and this bothered him.

"Our son plays jazz," said Mrs. Lewis. "I began teaching him piano when he was eight years old. Willie started him on trumpet when he was nine. He had a little band when he went to college. If it wasn't for that band, he would not have finished college. We couldn't afford the money. So you see," Mrs. Lewis said, "jazz music helped our boy get an education."

"He's got fifty men working under him," Willie added proudly. "He was always good in school."

"My teacher says I'm good in arithmetic," Tom B. offered.

"Keep it up, Tom B., and you'll go to college someday."

"Had enough to eat?" Mrs. Lewis asked. "Want another piece of pie?"

"No thank you, ma'am. I'm full."

"Let's play a couple of numbers for our guest, what do you say?" Willie asked his wife.

"Very well," she answered, "but only a couple. I've got to get those dishes washed."

They went into the living room. Mrs. Lewis sat on an old-fashioned piano bench and her fingers skipped nimbly over the keys, playing in several rolling chords. Willie took his trumpet from the case and Tom B. noticed that the mouthpiece was separate. Willie put it carefully into place. Mrs. Lewis hit several notes on the piano, and Willie tuned up by playing the same note

on the trumpet. He sounded a three-note musical phrase. Mrs. Lewis nodded, and Tom B. found himself tapping his feet to a rollicking jazz tune.

"What's that piece called?" Tom B. asked.

" 'Shake 'Em Up'," Willie replied.

They played church tunes that Tom B. knew. Mrs. Lewis sang "Take My Hand, Precious Lord" and "Sweet Bye and Bye." Tom B. sang softly to himself.

Mrs. Lewis said, "I've got to get my work done."

"Thank you for the music," Tom B. said.

"You're welcome." She went into the kitchen.

"I believe I'll have another cup of coffee," Willie said. He put the trumpet on the chair, after taking the mouthpiece out, and went to the kitchen.

Tom B., half afraid, touched the shiny brass of the horn. He looked quickly toward the kitchen door and pushed down the mother-of-pearl valve. He picked up the horn and held it to his lips. He could hear the band play, and he was playing too. Music filled his mind. The music was so real that he started to dance. As he turned toward the door, he saw Willie Lewis with a cup of steaming coffee in his hand and a grin on his face. Quickly Tom B. placed the trumpet back on the chair.

"You think you want to be a musician?" Willie asked in a quiet voice.

"Yes, sir," Tom B. answered softly.

Willie walked over to the piano. He rummaged around in the other trumpet case and brought out a mouthpiece. He handed it to Tom B. Willie put his own mouthpiece in the trumpet and pulled up a chair by the piano bench.

Tom B. was almost breathless. Here was Willie Lewis getting ready to show him how to play the trumpet. He could feel his heart pound with excitement.

"You know what we call this instrument?" Willie asked.

"Trumpet," replied Tom B.

"That's right. Are you right- or left-handed?"

"Right-handed."

"Here is the way you hold a trumpet." Willie said as he pressed it firmly to his lips. His right hand hovered over the three valves.

"When you blow, say 'too,' and blow from here." Willie patted his middle. "Feel my stomach," he said. He blew a loud note, and Tom B. felt Willie's hard and rigid stomach muscles.

"Now you try." Willie took his mouthpiece out. He showed Tom B. how to put the mouthpiece on exactly right. Tom B. put his lips to the trumpet. He blew, puffing his cheeks as if he had the mumps. He blew until spots danced before his eyes and his face grew red. He made a tinny squeak come out of the trumpet.

Willie didn't say anything. He watched for a few minutes. At last he said, "That's the way I started. I almost blew my insides out at first."

Tom B. was disappointed. "It won't blow for me."

"Sure it will," said Willie. "You don't know the trick of it yet. You'll learn. You see, you must force a column of air into the mouthpiece, and your lips must be toughened to take a lot of pressure. The tone is controlled with your lips and the air you blow into the horn. The valves

play the notes you want. Your lips will be mighty sore at first, and you need to keep in practice or your lips will not be able to control the tone. You've got to keep the lip up, as we say."

He took the trumpet from Tom B., put back his own mouthpiece, and filled the room with a clear steady tone. Then Willie took the mouthpiece out once more and blew into it without the trumpet. The sound was high-pitched, but the tone was loud and clear.

"I want you to practice with the mouthpiece," he said to Tom B. "Once you have learned to use your lips and stomach muscles instead of your cheeks, you'll be on your way. Don't forget to say 'too' as you blow. And be sure to practice."

Tom B. looked at the wooden clock on the wall. "I guess I'd better be going," he said slowly.

"Want me to drive you home?"

"I'll get me a bus."

"Go two blocks straight out the door and catch the Claiborne bus. It will take you downtown. Do you have money?"

"Yes, sir."

Willie called his wife into the living room. She gravely shook hands with Tom B.

"It was nice having you, Tom B. I'm going to expect you back."

"Thank you, ma'am. I'll be back. I sure liked the supper," he added.

Willie walked to the gate with him. "Call me up in a week, and we'll have another lesson."

Tom B. nodded happily. "I sure had a good time, Mr. Lewis."

Willie snapped his fingers. "I almost forgot. If you ever have time, go to the Jazz Museum at 1017 Dumaine Street. Say hello to my friend Clay Burke. He'll tell you a lot about New Orleans jazz, and there's plenty to see there. 1017 Dumaine. Well, good-by, Tom B., and I'll see you in a week or so."

Tom B. clutched the mouthpiece of the trumpet all the way downtown. He got off the bus at Canal Street, picked up his shoeshine box, and caught his bus in front of the Krauss Department Store. He did not put his precious trumpet mouthpiece in his pocket until he got to his front door.

5

The Unholy Noise

It was ten o'clock before Tom B. lazily opened his eyes the next morning. The delicious smell of buckwheat cakes made him hop out of bed and run into the kitchen. His grandmother was carefully dropping golden pancake batter into a sizzling pan. The table was set. A jug of his favorite syrup, blackstrap molasses, was by his plate.

"Morning, Mom," he said cheerfully as he sat down.

"What you doing setting down at the table without washing your face and hands?" his grandmother demanded.

How could she know that I didn't wash? he thought and hurriedly went to wash up.

When he came back, he sat down again without saying anything. He didn't quite know how to deal with his grandmother. He knew that she loved him and wanted everything good for him. But on the other hand, she was strict and often cranky. He liked her best when she only pretended to be angry. But sometimes it was hard to tell whether she was really angry or only pretending.

"I'm sorry I got up too late for Sunday school, Mom," he began carefully.

"That's all right," she answered. "You were sleeping so sound, I didn't have the heart to wake you up. You and me, we'll go to church."

She put three buckwheat cakes on his plate and poured a glass of milk. "Now, don't waste the molasses," she warned. "If I don't watch, you'll drown the buckwheat cakes and leave half the blackstrap on your plate."

He poured molasses on each pancake, and in a short time his plate was almost as clean as if it had been washed.

"Want more?" she asked, smiling with pleasure.

"Please, ma'am," he answered. Soon three more golden buckwheat cakes appeared on his plate.

His grandmother asked, "What did you do yesterday?"

"I was downtown and sort of around." He didn't look up from his plate.

"You didn't go round the docks, did you?" she questioned him sharply.

"No, ma'am." He looked straight at his grandmother. This seemed to satisfy her. She got up and made herself three pancakes. Neither said anything for the rest of the meal.

Tom B. finished his second helping, drank another glass of milk, and left the table with a sigh of satisfaction.

"Take your bath and get dressed for church," his grandmother said.

In thirty minutes Tom B. was dressed in his blue suit, white shirt, and red bow tie. He carefully put his mouthpiece in his coat pocket and went outside to wait for his grandmother. She soon appeared, dressed in a gleaming white uniform, white shoes and stockings, and a stiffly starched white nurse's cap.

Tom B. felt proud, walking to church with his grandmother. It was an honor to be a deaconess. Such a position was given to ladies who helped the church in many ways. Men doffed their hats as they greeted her along the way. People spoke to her with great respect.

The church was a small brick building with a Sunday school room attached to the back. A white wooden bell tower rose above the red brick. Two ushers wearing white gloves and red flowers in their lapels greeted them at the door.

"Good morning, Mrs. Williams. Morning, Tom B.," an usher said.

"Morning," Tom B. answered. His grandmother nodded and smiled.

"Lovely morning." The usher handed them a program.

"Sure is," Tom B. agreed. They were led to a seat, but Tom B. saw a friend farther toward the front.

"Mom, can I please set with Alex?"

"All right," she answered, "but mind you, no noise."

"We won't make no noise."

His friend Alex greeted him. Tom B. looked back to see if his grandmother was watching, but she was whispering to a lady next to her.

The Reverend George Leander Barnett sat in an imposing chair behind the pulpit. He was a large man, and his eyes darted here and there as he watched the members of his congregation come into the church. He wore a red carnation in the lapel of his black suit. A black tie stood out against his white shirt. A heavy gold watch chain hung across his vest.

A lady in a black choir robe was seated at a small electric organ, and when the minister nodded she played softly. Some of the members started singing. Tom B. knew the song. It was "Leaning on the Everlasting Arms." The choir came in and took its place on the platform behind the minister. The minister nodded, and the choir sang "Do, Lord, Remember Me."

Mr. Barnett slowly walked to the pulpit. He said, "Good morning, children."

The whole congregation answered, "Good morning, Preacher."

"It's a good morning. Say Amen."

"Amen," the congregation answered.

"We had a fine Sunday school today. Fine Sunday school. Not everybody who should have come got here. Overslept, I guess."

Tom B. felt that Mr. Barnett was looking directly at him. He squirmed in his seat. He looked for his grandmother, but she was now on a bench against the wall with the other deaconesses. She was watching the minister.

Mr. Barnett went on, "And now Brother Larry Rockmore will offer a prayer."

A slim man came to the center and knelt on one knee. He prayed for the forgiveness of sins. He thanked God for being good to the people of the congregation for another week. He prayed for His blessings on all. As he prayed, someone started humming. Others took up the melody until his prayers were accompanied by the soft music of many voices. He asked God's blessings on all His white children and ended by praying for a world of peace and brotherhood.

The minister said, "Amen." The congregation answered with "Amen." He announced, "The choir will sing 'God's Word Shall Never Pass Away.'" After the third stanza, the whole congregation joined in the singing.

"Let everybody say Amen," repeated Mr. Barnett.

"Amen," the congregation answered.

More songs were sung and more prayers offered. The prayers seemed too long to Tom B. His neck got tired from bowing his head.

Then Mr. Barnett said, "A special offering will be taken for the children of the Magnolia Orphanage. I ask that you be as generous as you can." The organ played softly, and the ushers passed wooden plates with green felt bottoms. While the plates were being passed, Mr. Barnett said, "I sometimes think the old songs are the best. We have been singing the old ones today, the ones that we remember from childhood. It's good to hear the songs that our mothers and fathers sang. Let us sing another, this time without the organ." And he started singing "Who Will Be a Witness for My Lord?"

The congregation and choir made the church ring. Tom B. sang as loudly as he could, enjoying every note.

"We had a shouting in the camp," said the minister.

"Yes, yes," the people answered.

"And now," he said, opening a large Bible on the pulpit, "I take today's text from The Book of Ezekiel, chapter 37, verses 1 to 11." He read the Bible verses and closed the book with a flourish. His sermon retold the reading from The Book of Ezekiel with many examples from everyday life. Tom B. understood most of what the preacher said. His voice rose higher and higher. The excitement of the congregation mounted with every word.

He shouted, "Son of Man, can these bones live? Say Amen."

"Amen," the congregation roared.

The sermon ended. Someone started singing "Them Bones." Tom B. threw back his head and sang with the rest,

> "Well, the toe bone jump to the foot bone,
> The foot bone jump to the ankle bone,
> The ankle bone jump to the leg bone,
> Them bones, them bones, them jumping bones."

He was so excited that he could hardly sit still. He clapped his hands to the music, along with most of the congregation. Reaching into his pocket, he brought out the trumpet mouthpiece. He blew into it easily, so that it would not make any noise. The rhythm of the music rocked the little church. Suddenly Tom B. was no longer in church. He was playing "Them Bones" on the trumpet with Willie Lewis. He did not hear the song end or the minister say, "Let us pray."

The church was absolutely quiet. All were waiting for the words of their pastor, their heads bowed. Tom B., his

mind still running wild with the music, gave one final blow.

A loud shrill blast cut into the silence. People jumped. Ladies screamed. A few laughed. All looked toward Tom B. He sat frozen in his seat for what seemed like an hour. He stared straight ahead, wishing the floor would swallow him.

Then he heard his grandmother's voice say quietly, "I think we had better go."

He looked up. She was standing in the aisle beside him, a look of shocked disbelief on her face.

Turning, she walked slowly toward the door. Tom B., his head down, followed. As he walked out, he heard the voice of Mr. Barnett in prayer. His feeling of shame was almost more than he could stand.

6

Hooky

His grandmother would not speak to him. Tom B. knew he had hurt her cruelly. He wanted to tell her how sorry he was, but he was too full of shame. Instead, he went to his room and stayed there the rest of the day. When he went to the kitchen at suppertime, food was on the table, but his grandmother was in her room. Her bedroom door was closed. When Tom B. tried to eat, the lump in his throat would not let the food go down. He wanted to cry, but no tears came. When he went back to his room, he lay on the bed looking at the ceiling. It was hours before he fell asleep.

The next morning he got into his jeans and blue-checked shirt and went into the kitchen. Breakfast was on the table.

"Good morning, Mom," he said softly. She looked at him, but said nothing.

He grew uncomfortable. Suddenly he blurted out, "I didn't mean to make noise, Mom, honest. It just came out."

At last she spoke. "I suppose you know that you shamed me in front of everybody in the church."

Tom B. could not look her in the eye.

"What kind of thing made that terrible racket?" she asked with a quiver in her voice.

"It's a mouthpiece of a trumpet," he answered.

"How did you come by it?"

"Willie Lewis loaned it to me."

"That jazz musician?" Her body stiffened and her mouth grew tight and grim.

Tom B. took a deep breath. "I went to a jazz parade, Mom. It was the Eureka Brass Band and Willie Lewis is the leader. He took me home to lunch and I met Mrs. Lewis. They're nice folks, Mom, honest." His look pleaded for understanding.

"Nice, indeed," was all his grandmother said, but there was deep scorn in her voice.

"And they told me about how their boy went to college and played jazz music so he could get money for school." Then Tom B. thought of something else. "Mr. Lewis is a deacon in Gloryland Baptist Church."

This bit of news caught Mrs. Williams by surprise. "A deacon?"

"We said grace at the table, the same grace you say."

Her look hardened. "That doesn't make any difference. The church is full of hypocrites. How come he loaned you the mouthpiece?"

"I guess it's because I told him I wanted to learn to play the trumpet," said Tom B. with a sinking heart.

"You go and get that thing and bring it here," she said grimly.

When he came back, she took it out of his hand. As her fingers closed over the mouthpiece, Tom B. wondered

what he would say to Willie. He went to his room and waited until schooltime. The more he thought about her taking the mouthpiece, the angrier he became.

"She didn't have no right to do that," he raged. "That mouthpiece belongs to Willie Lewis. It's not fair."

He heard the door close, and he knew that his grandmother had gone to work without telling him good-by. He looked at the clock. It was almost time to go to school.

"To hell with school," he said out loud. "I'm going downtown."

He caught the bus and got off at Canal Street. The shops were getting ready for the day's customers. Some men swept sidewalks and others washed windows. Empty boxes were piled close to the curb awaiting the trashman. A delicious odor came to Tom B. from the five-and-ten. He watched a man make doughnuts in the window. The door was open, but a chain was stretched across the doorway.

"Mister, can I get me a couple of doughnuts?" he asked.

"Sorry, Sonny," the man answered. "We don't open till nine forty-five."

Disappointed, Tom B. walked down to the river at the foot of Canal Street. The sight of the twin towers of the Algiers ferry gave him an idea. He decided to take a ride across the river. It was free. As he got to the top of the steps to the waiting room he saw only six people waiting for the ferry. Four cars were waiting on the ramp leading to the wharf.

Three sharp whistles blew. The boat grumbled up to

the dock. Tom B. watched as it slowly and carefully ranged itself along the wharf. He admired the skill of the captain in the pilot house. Tom B. walked onto the top deck of the ferry and watched the cars come down the ramp and circle the deck.

He walked down the stairs to the main deck and watched the deckhands unwind the big ropes from the steel cleat that held the ferry close to the wharf. Soon the whistle blew again, and Tom B. ran to the stern and watched the big wheel churn the water. The boat backed away from the wharf and swung out into the river.

He saw a large cargo ship at the nearby Poydras Street docks, and he decided to watch the loading when he got back. He thought about his grandmother's orders to stay away from the docks, but he did not care.

The brown water of the broad Mississippi River slapped at the sides of the ferry as it chugged to the other side. Tom B. enjoyed seeing the ships that waited to take on or unload cargo. He said over and over to himself in a singsong voice, "Mississippi River, Mississippi River, Mississippi River." The long bridge crossed to his right, its steel girders jutting across the skyline. It was alive with cars going back and forth.

They look like dime-store toys, he said to himself.

Someone touched him roughly on the shoulder. He whirled around and saw one of the deckhands looking at him with unfriendly eyes.

"Which one is your car, boy?" he asked angrily. Tom B. did not answer.

"I say, which one is your car?" the man repeated.

Tom B. walked past him to the top deck.

"Stay up there where you belong, you hear? Ain't nobody allowed down here 'less he's in a car," the man shouted at Tom B.

The whistle blew as they neared the Algiers side of the river. Tom B. watched, fascinated, while the pilot and deckhands skillfully brought the ferry snugly against the wharf. Tom B. stayed on the boat, and in thirty minutes the ferry was back on the New Orleans side of the river.

He wandered over to the Poydras Street docks and sat on one of the steel cleats to watch a large machine at work in the river. A group of rafts were connected to the machine and long sections of pipe lay along the top of the rafts. Something that looked like a gigantic screw turned in the water very close to the wharf. Muddy water shot out of a pipe at the end of one of the rafts farther out in the river.

A man stood nearby, also watching the machine.

"What's that boat doing?" Tom B. asked.

"That's a dredge," was the reply. "It is clearing the mud away from the bottom near the dock so that the water will be deep enough for the big ships to load and unload their cargoes."

"How does it do that?"

"The pipe sucks the loose mud from the bottom of the river and throws it out where the river is deeper."

"Thank you," said Tom B.

He watched the river workers on the dredge scurrying about in their bright-orange life jackets. The brown water of the river swirled in an evil way as he watched it twist and turn.

"Man, I'd hate to fall in. Must be a thousand feet deep," he said.

"Not quite," the man laughed. "The river is about forty feet deep by the docks and around a hundred feet out in the middle."

When Tom B. tired of watching the dredging, he walked over to a ship tied to the dock. It was a freighter named the *North Star*. Bits of rust clung to the ship near the waterline. On the upper deck he noticed laundry hung on a short line. Along with men's shirts and trousers were diapers and other articles of baby clothing. This puzzled him.

Men moved about the dock, each busy with some task. One drove a small cart with two prongs sticking out in front. Tom B. watched him go to a small wooden platform piled high with old car radiators and pull a lever. The prongs lifted the platform and radiators. The cart wheeled around and put down the load at the edge of the dock. Two men placed a wire rope around the radiators. One motioned to the sky with his thumb, and the radiators were lifted high into the air by a crane on the ship. Another man used hand signals to guide the radiators to the hold of the ship, where other men were waiting. Tom B. could hear the voices of other men in the hold, arranging the cargo.

On the dock a crippled man stood by a group of small barrels painted brown, blue, and orange. A box of paper cups was nearby. Workers came often to the barrels for a drink of cold water. Tom B. suddenly found he was thirsty.

"Mister," he asked, "can I have a drink of water, please?"

"Help yourself," the man said, and he gave Tom B. a cup. The water was cold. Tom B. drank four cups before he was satisfied.

"Mister," Tom B. asked, "how come those baby diapers hanging up there on the boat?"

The man laughed. "It's a ship, not a boat, and the captain of the *North Star* brought his wife and kid over from England."

Tom B. liked the man. "Why they loading the old radiators?"

"Those old radiators are worth money," the man said, "because there is a lot of copper in them. They will be shipped to Japan and used in factories."

Tom B. saw that the wire rope was not all the way around one group of radiators. "Mister," he shouted, but the noise of the crane engine drowned out his voice. The radiators hovered over the wide opening of the hold. The wire suddenly slipped off. There was a terrible crash. Loud voices, some of them swear words, came from the hold.

"Anybody hurt?"

"Nobody hurt," came an answering call, "but for God's sake be careful."

After watching for a long time, Tom B. grew restless. He decided to have a look inside the huge warehouse. A big sign by the door said Keep Down Accidents. No one was around, so Tom B. walked into the warehouse. It was the biggest room he could ever have imagined. It seemed to stretch on for miles. There were boxes marked CHEESE FOR BRAZIL. Large sacks of flour were marked GIFT OF THE UNITED STATES GOVERNMENT. There were oyster shells from Louisiana bound for Asia. There was so much to see that his head swam. It was fun to go from stack to stack to see where things came from and where they were going.

"Hey, you, boy!" a shout interrupted his fun. Someone walked toward him. "Come here, boy!"

Tom B. backed away. He didn't think he had done anything wrong, but he was frightened. He started running. The dock worker ran after him, blowing a whistle. This frightened Tom B. more. He dodged, panic-stricken, between high stacks of boxes. Other men came running. He saw a door in a far corner of the warehouse, and he made for it, running at top speed. The guards were a few feet from him when he reached the door. He pulled at the door, but it was stuck. Desperate, he jerked and tugged. Suddenly without warning the door opened. He leaped out into the sunshine with the guards right behind him. One of them chased him as far as the railroad tracks. Then he gave up and went back to the warehouse. Tom B. did not stop running until he was on Canal Street. Exhausted, he sat down in the shade of a building to rest.

7

The Jazz Museum

The noon whistle blew, its shrill tones echoing up and down Canal Street. Tom B. was hungry. He had forgotten to take money, and all that he had in his pocket was a dime.

"Man, I got to get me some money," he said to himself, but he wasn't really worried. Whistling, he walked up Canal Street to Royal Street in the French Quarter. Tourists were beginning to make the rounds of the gift shops, antique stores, and art galleries along the street. It was easy for Tom B. to spot a tourist. Window-shopping and a camera around the neck were the signs.

He walked up to a man and woman looking into the window of an antique store. "Hey, take my picture for a quarter," he said.

The man grinned with the usual good cheer of a person on vacation. "What would I do with your picture?"

"Show it to your friends," Tom B. answered promptly. "I come from a famous New Orleans family. My grandpa used to own the whole French Quarter." It was a wild fib. He knew that the man would not believe him, but he hoped that he would be amused enough to give him some money.

"O.K.," said the tourist. "Stand over here." He motioned Tom B. to stand beside a horse and carriage by the curb.

"Do you mind if I take your picture with the boy?" the tourist asked the driver, an old man dressed in a long-tailed coat, black trousers, and a black top hat.

"No, sir," the driver answered. With an eye for business he asked, "Let me take you and the lady on a buggy tour of the French Quarter."

"First let's have the picture," answered the tourist. Tom B. posed with the driver. "Say 'cheese,'" ordered the photographer. Tom B. gave a wide grin. The man handed Tom B. a quarter and said, "I'm glad to have met a member of a famous family."

Tom B. walked on. There were many tourists in the French Quarter now. He wished he had brought his shoeshine box. He had an idea. He took his handkerchief out of his pocket and went up to a group of men standing in front of the Louisiana Wildlife Museum.

"Shine, Mister?" he asked one of them.

"No, thanks."

"Man, those shoes are dusty," he persisted.

"They will only get dirty again," the man answered. "Besides, where is your shoeshine box?"

"I gives them a special shine with a pure linen rag," said Tom B. He didn't wait, but kneeled down and ordered, "Put your foot on my leg."

The tourist, with a rueful smile, gave up and did as

instructed. Tom B. shined the shoe vigorously.

"Now the other one." The man obliged.

Tom B. looked at the shoes and said, "Man, that's some shine. Ought to be worth more than a quarter." He looked at the man out of the corners of his eyes.

His friends laughed. One of them said, "Bill, you've just been taken by an expert."

The man called Bill cheerfully dug into his pocket and brought out a half-dollar.

"Young man," he said solemnly, "keep that up and one day you'll be a millionaire."

"I don't want to be a millionaire. I want to be a musician," replied Tom B.

"The way you work, you'll make it," the tourist said.

It was almost noon, and Tom B.'s stomach was growling. He walked to Canal Street and bought a hamburger and root beer at the five-and-ten. Suddenly he remembered that at this very time he should be eating a peanut-butter-and-jelly sandwich at school. A bad feeling came over him, a something that he could not explain. He thought about the trumpet mouthpiece, and silent anger flared against his grandmother.

She don't care about me, he thought. She didn't even fix my lunch today.

He strolled over to Burgundy Street. This was a pleasant street, a neighborhood where people lived in old-fashioned tiny houses packed together so that only a narrow entryway led to the back. It was warm, and people sat outside on chairs trying to catch a little breeze. Many of the old houses were gone, and new apartment buildings rose in their places. Tom B. didn't like the new apartments. They were a fancy copy of the old homes and somehow they seemed wrong. A thought came to him.

Why not visit the Jazz Museum? He went up to a worker pouring cement for one of the apartment houses.

"Mister, where is the Jazz Museum?"

"Go up Burgundy four blocks to Dumaine, turn left, and keep walking a few blocks. You'll see it."

Tom B. nodded his thanks. He found Dumaine Street easily. The houses along Dumaine were like those on Burgundy but newer. He walked until he came to a red brick building that looked different from the houses on the street. A metal sign on the outside proclaimed NEW ORLEANS JAZZ MUSEUM. Tom B. went to the shuttered door but he saw another sign that made him stop. It said ADMISSION TWENTY-FIVE CENTS.

I ain't going to pay no quarter, he said to himself. He opened the door carefully. A bell tinkled. A round-faced man looked up from behind a glass showcase. He was a pudgy man with clear blue eyes and a bristly red mustache. Tom B. approached him warily.

"What do you want?" the man asked, a note of suspicion in his voice.

"Nothing," Tom B. answered.

"We don't have any." Tom B. giggled. The man looked at him for a moment and said, "Was that funny?"

"Yes, sir."

"I like a good audience." The man almost smiled. "What are you doing here?"

"I wants to see the things in the Jazz Museum," Tom B. replied quickly.

"Well, that's different," the man said. "Did you see the sign on the door?"

"Yes, sir."

"What does it say?"

"It say, 'Admission Twenty-five Cents.' "

"Well?"

Tom B. looked at the ceiling, playing for time. He had decided to pay the twenty-five cents because he really wanted to see the museum, but he waited to see what the man would do next.

"The Jazz Museum needs money," said the man with a frown. "We can't let people come in here for nothing."

Tom B. noticed that the man was having a hard time keeping from smiling, even though he sounded gruff.

"Willie Lewis told me that I should ought to come here and learn about jazz," Tom B. said casually.

The man seemed surprised. "Willie Lewis! Do you know my friend Willie Lewis?"

Tom B. nodded happily. "Do I knows him? I ate at his house last Saturday. Sure I knows him, And he's going to teach me trumpet."

The man whistled. "Well, I'm impressed." He came from behind the showcase. "My name is Clay Burke, and I'm the curator of the New Orleans Jazz Museum, the only museum in the world devoted entirely to New Orleans jazz," he added proudly.

" 'Curator,' what's that?" Tom B. asked.

"I run the place," Clay answered. They shook hands.

"And what is your name?" grinned Clay.

"My name is Thomas Boynton Fraser."

"That's a mouthful of a name. What do they call you?"

"They calls me Tom B."

"That's better. All right, Tom B., consider yourself a guest of the New Orleans Jazz Museum, owned and operated by the famous New Orleans Jazz Club. Any friend of Willie Lewis is a friend of mine."

"Thank you," replied Tom B. There was more than a hint of triumph in his voice.

"Young man, let the grand tour begin," Clay said with a wave of his hand. He stopped in front of some colorful posters. "These posters are from concerts given by New Orleans musicians in countries all over the world. See, here is one from Poland, and Denmark, and Japan. There are New Orleans jazz fans just about every place."

"Mr. Jackson at Preservation Hall told me the same thing," Tom B. said.

"Oh, you know Allan Jackson. You really get around." Clay went on, "Here is the Tree of Jazz showing how this kind of music developed over hundreds of years." He showed Tom B. a large showcase with the sign ORIGIN OF THE BANJO.

Tom B. stopped in front of a case and looked at a battered cornet.

Clay said, "Here, let me show you something." He opened the case and tenderly drew out the cornet. "This cornet," he said softly, "belonged to Louis when he lived in New Orleans."

Tom B. didn't think much of the battered old horn.

"Is a cornet the same as a trumpet?" he asked.

Clay sounded impatient. "The trumpet is harder to play, and the cornet has a little mellower tone. But see here, Tom B., when I said 'Louis,' I meant Louis Armstrong, the greatest musician to come out of New Orleans. He has played New Orleans music in Europe, Asia, and Africa. He is probably the best-known musician in all the world. And he learned to play cornet when he wasn't much older than you are right now."

Clay handed the cornet to Tom B. Now it looked important. Tom B. trembled a little as he held it in his hands. He handed it back carefully and whispered, "Thanks."

Clay walked over to some dial telephones on the wall. "Here is something you'll like. Listen," he said. He took the receiver from the hook and put it on Tom B.'s ear. Then he dialed a number. The sound of New Orleans jazz came through the phone.

"Man, oh, man!" shouted Tom B.

"I thought you'd like it," said Clay. "You go ahead and listen for a while. I've got some work to do in the back." He showed Tom B. how to get different kinds of jazz music by dialing different numbers.

Tom B. settled down to listen. He heard marching bands, small combos, clarinet, piano, and banjo solos. He saved music featuring the trumpet for last. He heard a recording of Willie Lewis playing "Bourbon Street Parade." He could tell it was Willie because of the way it sounded—a special Willie Lewis way. It was wonderful. Tom B. couldn't sit still. First he tapped his feet.

Then he got up from the bench and started dancing. He danced faster and faster until suddenly the music stopped. The broken cord of the receiver dangled in his hand.

He looked toward the back of the museum and saw Clay coming from his office. Tom B. didn't wait. He started running to the front door.

"Hey, where are you going in such a hurry?" Clay called. Tom B. ran blindly, paying no attention. He didn't see the wire rack filled with paperback books. Blam, he ran into the rack. It tottered for a few seconds and fell with a crash. Books spilled out in every direction.

Tom B. jumped over the rack and reached the door. Clay tried to jump over the rack too, but his foot caught in the wire, and he fell to the floor. Tom B. jerked the door open and the bells jingled madly as he slammed it shut and ran out into the street.

"Oh, Lord, what did I do?" he mumbled as he ran in terror. He thought he heard Clay yell something like, "Tom B., come back," but that only made him run faster. Clay must be furious at him for breaking things in the museum.

Tom B. ran until he got to Royal Street, looking back now and then to see if Clay was still following. He was safe. Out of breath and sweating heavily from heat and fear, he sat down in the shade. He was sure that he would never be allowed in the Jazz Museum again.

8

Back to the Hall

As Tom B. rested he talked to himself. I didn't mean to knock the books over. The man came running after me like he was going to clobber me. I was scared. He thought about Clay. He seemed all right, and I liked him. I held Louis Armstrong's cornet. Wow! Tom B. sighed. He wished that he could go back to the Museum.

He walked toward Bourbon Street. Little heat waves danced in the sunlight. Sweat rolled down into his eyes, and his shirt was wet from running. He put his handkerchief around his shirt collar, but it didn't help much. When he came to St. Peter Street, he walked until he came to Preservation Hall. The iron gates were locked. It looked cool and inviting inside.

He rattled the gates and shouted, "Mr. Jackson, Mr. Jackson!"

"Coming," a voice from the Hall answered. Allan came out to the gate.

"Hi, Tom B.," he said. "What are you doing downtown this time of day?"

"They's a teachers meeting, so we don't have school," Tom B. lied.

"Do you want to come in and help me for a while? I'm sweeping out the place and getting ready for to-night."

"Sure do," Tom B. answered. Allan gave him the broom, and soon he stirred up a dust. He placed the chairs and benches in order and dusted each one. When he was finished, he went to the entryway. Allan was placing phonograph records on the rack.

"What next?" Tom B. asked.

Allan laughed. "You sure an eager beaver. Come back to the patio, and we'll see if there is something for you to do."

The patio was beautiful. There was a small fishpond in a shaded corner. Metal furniture stood under a huge banana tree, and some beautiful shiny dark church pews stretched along the brick wall of the apartment. The old, old bricks of the building were different shades of brown, white, and red.

"How about sweeping the patio, and then we'll have some lemonade in the apartment."

"O.K.," Tom B. answered. Once again he made the dust fly. He worked hard, and in thirty minutes he had finished the job. Timidly he knocked on the door of the apartment.

"Come in," called Sandra's voice. It was cool inside. The high brick walls were covered with paintings. A couch was piled with phonograph records. A tall book-case, filled with books and records and some kind of ancient statues, covered one whole end of the room. Wooden steps led up to a balcony.

"Hi, Tom B.," Sandra said warmly.

"Hey," he answered. He felt shy in front of her.

"Please sit down and make yourself at home," she invited. "Will you have some lemonade?"

"If you please."

She brought in three tall glasses. The sweet-sour taste of the lemonade was cool and good. Allan put a record on the stereo. It was Willie Lewis and his band playing "Back of Town Blues."

Tom B. enjoyed the music, but he was so tired from the excitement of the day that he could not keep from yawning. His head nodded in spite of all that he could do. Sandra noticed.

"Why don't you lie down and rest for a few minutes?" she invited.

He smiled thankfully and in a moment he was asleep.

Two and a half hours later Tom B. was awakened by Sandra, who was patting him gently on the shoulder. He sat up and rubbed his eyes.

"Sleep well?" she asked.

"Sure did," he grinned. "What time is it?"

"Almost six. Hungry?"

"Yes, ma'am!" he said. Allan came from the kitchen carrying a large tray, with three large Cokes and two good-sized loaves of bread. He cut the bread into halves and handed a section to Tom B. It was a giant of a sandwich, and it smelled delicious.

"Man, what a san'wich!" exclaimed Tom B.

"This is the famous Italian Po' Boy Sandwich from Central Grocery," said Allan.

Tom B. lifted the top piece of bread and his eyes

grew wide. Salami, cheese, salad, pickles, relish, olives, and two other kinds of meat were all nestled between halves of the soft white Italian bread.

"Dig in," Allan said. Tom B. held the sandwich in both hands, looked at it thoughtfully, opened his mouth as wide as it would go, and took a huge bite. It was the best sandwich he had ever tasted, and he did not stop eating until it disappeared.

"Want more?" Sandra asked.

"You really can put food away," grinned Allan.

"I might try another small piece," Tom B. replied. Sandra handed him a generous part of the other sandwich. He ate, but more slowly this time.

"That food's good." Tom B. washed down the last bit with a drink of Coke.

"I believe I owe you this for your work," said Allan, and he handed Tom B. a dollar.

Tom B. looked at the bill as if he didn't believe it. He tried to give it back to Allan. "I don't want pay for helping you out, Mr. Jackson. Besides you gave me my supper and," he thought fast, "maybe you'll let me listen to the music tonight."

Allan and Sandra looked at each other. She said, "O.K., but when we tell you it's time to go home, you must go. We don't want you to stay out too late."

"O.K.," said Tom B. He looked at some magazines while Sandra washed the dishes and Allan wrote letters. It was getting dark, and the tourists were beginning their evening stroll in the French Quarter. Allan, Sandra, and Tom B. went to the Hall together. The musicians came in, carrying their instruments and chatting with each other. Tom B. saw Willie Lewis come into the Hall.

"Hey, Mr. Lewis."

"Hey, Tom B. You practicing on that mouthpiece?"

Tom B. didn't answer the question exactly. He said, "I blew it good and loud once."

"Blowing loud isn't learning to play. You've got to learn to blow soft too," Willie said.

"Yes, sir," answered Tom B., hoping there would be no more questions.

"I'll be looking for you next Saturday for your lesson," said Willie. "Come before noon. Mrs. Lewis wants you to eat with us."

Tom B. nodded. He was miserable, but he could not bring himself to tell Willie about the trouble with his grandmother.

Soon the musicians began to tune up. It was a pleasant sound to Tom B. They chatted as they got ready to play, and Tom B. listened to every word.

Willie said, "Oh, yes, he died day before yesterday. They are laying him away tomorrow."

"Where's the funeral?"

"From the church at 8th and Danneel Street."

"What time, noon?"

"That's right," answered Willie.

"Whose band they got?" asked Jim.

"Just a pickup band."

"Are they marching to the graveyard?"

"Clear to the graveyard, fourteen blocks there and fourteen blocks back," Willie said.

"You working, Willie?" the drummer asked.

"Yes, indeed. I'll be there with my trumpet on. He was my friend, and I'm doing it for the family."

"No loot?" one of the musicians laughed.

"That's right."

Tom B. itched with curiosity. He only half understood what they were saying. He walked to Allan.

"Mr. Jackson, the mens are talking about a funeral. What funeral?"

"Oh, that," answered Allan. "A musician died the other day, and a band will play music for his funeral. It's a way that respect is paid to the memory of one who has died."

"Can I go?"

"You'll be in school," answered Allan, "unless the teachers meeting is still going on." He looked straight at Tom B. Tom B. turned his eyes away and walked back into the Hall.

Allan opened the iron gates, and the tourists came in, dropping dollars into Sandra's basket. Allan looked at his watch and nodded to Willie. He put his trumpet to his lips and played three notes. He tapped his right foot twice, and the evening of jazz music began with "Bill Bailey, Won't You Please Come Home." Tom B. was happy again. The crowd gave out with hand-clapping, foot-tapping, and smiles of joy.

Later in the evening Allan motioned for Tom B. to come out to the gate. "Would you go up to the Bourbon House on the corner and get three cups of coffee for the musicians? Willie likes one spoon of sugar and no cream.

Percy wants no sugar and one cream, and Jim wants three spoons of sugar and one cream. Think you can remember that?"

"Sure can," he replied as Allan handed him some money.

Tom B. ran to the Bourbon House feeling quite important. "Three coffees for Allan at Preservation Hall," he said. He repeated the order.

"Jim sure likes his coffee sweet," said the waiter. "I wonder if all trombone players are like that?" He poured the coffee in paper cups, put lids on them, and placed the three in a paper sack. Tom B. paid and ran back to the Hall.

"That's fast service," said Allan.

Jim smiled and asked, "What are you going to be when you grow up?"

"A musician like Mr. Lewis," Tom B. came right back.

Time went by too fast. At nine forty-five Sandra beckoned for him to come out to the gate. "It's getting late, Tom B. I think you ought to go home."

"Yes, ma'am," he said, and he turned to go. Then he remembered his manners. "Thank you for the supper and the music."

"Good night, Tom B. Come back," Allan said.

He wandered around aimlessly for a while. At last he walked over to his bus stop and waited. A bus drew up, and he started to climb on. But he changed his mind.

As he paused on the steps of the bus, the driver said in an annoyed tone, "Get on or get off."

Tom B. got off the bus. He would not go home yet.

He looked up and down Canal Street. The blaze of light from the marquees of movie theaters and stores faded into a glitter of white, green, red, and amber colors, all mingled together.

Canal Street looks like a Christmas tree, thought Tom B. to himself. He walked toward the Civic Center and soon found himself in front of the public library. Floodlights made strange patterns on the black aluminum grillwork that framed the modern library building. Tom B. walked across the library lawn to the statue of George Washington. He could see the white outlines of City Hall and the State Supreme Court Building. A floodlight shone brightly on the parking lot behind the library. There were three cars in the lot. No one was around. Tom B. went over to one car and tried the door. It was unlocked. Crawling into the backseat, he curled up his tired body. He was soon asleep.

9

The Sorrowful Noise

Tom B. was wakened by the rumble of a bus coming into the station next door. The morning air was chilly. He shivered. The backseat had been long enough for him, but not wide enough. He felt stiff and sore.

He walked down the alley to Tulane Avenue. When he came to the Continental Bus station, he washed up, went into the lunchroom, and sat down at the counter.

"Watcha want?" a waitress asked in a peevish voice.

"A sweet roll and a glass of milk, please."

She watched him eat. "You're up awfully early," she said suspiciously.

"Yes, ma'am," he answered.

"Are you going to school early? You live around here?"

Tom B. didn't answer. He smiled. She went to another customer.

He was still hungry. "Can I have another roll, please?"

She brought it to him. "How come you're not eating breakfast at home?"

"My mamma forgot to buy milk last night," he answered quickly. This seemed to satisfy the waitress.

When he finished breakfast, he paid the cashier and went out into the morning air without any plan. Walking, he came to the back entrance of Charity Hospital. Its huge bulk loomed above him. Hospital workers, nurses, and doctors hurried through enormous doors. The building seemed to swallow people.

Tom B. sat down by a little hamburger stand nearby and watched the activity. It was a new, exciting world. He heard a siren several blocks away. In a few minutes the ambulance turned down Gravier Street and shot up the ramp to the emergency door of the hospital.

Two men in white uniform quickly but gently took an old man out of the ambulance, placed him on a bed with wheels, and rolled him through the big doors. This was a mystery to Tom B. Where did they go?

He saw young men in tan coats scurry back and forth across the street. "Are these men doctors?" Tom B. asked the man at the hamburger stand.

"No, they're medical students studying to be doctors. They study across the street, but they also work in the Charity Hospital."

People started coming to a door marked DISPENSARY. Both men and women waited in line, but there were more women than men. Many of the women carried babies in their arms.

"Who are these people?" Tom B. asked.

"They are waiting for medicine," was the answer.

Taxicabs lined up in the street in front of the hospital. When people came out, a police officer blew on a whistle, and a taxicab drove up the ramp.

"Are those folks going home?" Tom B. asked.

"That's right."

Tom B. watched for a long time. He felt sorry for the people who were brought to the hospital. He saw fear in the faces of many, especially the older people. All of those who got into taxicabs looked happy.

"I wonder what it's like to be in a hospital?" he mused.

The day was getting warm. Tom B. decided to go to Preservation Hall. Maybe the Jacksons would let him sit in their cool apartment and look at some magazines and listen to jazz records. The French Quarter was bulging with tourists. When he got to the Hall, he found the gates locked. He started to call Allan, but he noticed a police car cross St. Peter Street going up Bourbon. What if the police car would come around Royal Street and down St. Peter. Tom B. grew uneasy. Did his grandmother ask the police to look for him? Something told him to hide just in case. He ducked into the doorway next to the Hall.

An automobile did stop in front of the Hall, and Tom B. heard the gates rattle.

Then he heard Allan's voice, "Yes, officer?"

"I'm Officer Russell. Do you know of a shoeshine boy who hangs around Preservation Hall?"

"We have several boys who come here," Tom B. heard Allan say. "They change their silver money into dollar bills."

"This particular one didn't go home last night, and his grandmother is upset, according to the report that just reached us. His name is —"

Allan broke in, "Tom B. didn't go home? My wife sent him home a little before ten last night. Sure we know him. He ate with us. That kid is crazy about jazz music."

"It sounds like the same boy. Have a look at his picture."

"That's Tom B., all right," Allan said. "He's a good kid, though. I'd vouch for it."

"Good kid or not, his grandmother wants him home. Let us know if he shows up," said the officer.

"Certainly," answered Allan.

Tom B. hid behind the doorway until the police car drove away. I can't even go to Preservation Hall no more, he thought bitterly. He was angry at Allan. "I thought he was my friend," he said to himself sadly.

Tom B. wanted to get out of the French Quarter. All at once he remembered the funeral. The police wouldn't be there for sure. And if Allan and Sandra came, he would stay out of their way. Besides, his friend Willie Lewis would be there.

He stopped a man on Canal Street. "How do I get to 8th and Danneel, please?"

"Take the St. Charles streetcar. The conductor will tell you how to get there."

Tom B. crossed the street to the St. Charles streetcar, the last of the old-fashioned trolley cars in New Orleans. He told the conductor, "I want to go to 8th and Danneel, please."

"Get off at Louisiana Avenue and walk to the right," said the conductor.

Tom B. sat by an open window. It was his first ride

on a streetcar. He enjoyed the "ding ding" and "clang clang" of the motorman's bell as the streetcar ponderously got under way. In about fifteen minutes the conductor called Louisiana Avenue, and Tom B. got off the streetcar. He found 8th and Danneel easily.

Many people stood outside the church talking quietly. Tom B. heard the singing inside the church. Next he heard the voice of the minister preaching the sermon. A car drove up, and several musicians, Willie Lewis among them, got out of the car. Willie had a small bag of music slung over his shoulder. Tom B. remembered the painting in Preservation Hall.

He ran up to the musician. "Hey, Mr. Lewis," he said.

"Why aren't you in school, young man?" Willie demanded.

"Teachers meeting," replied Tom B. "When do the funeral start?"

"In a little while," Willie answered.

"I guess the funeral music is in the little bag," said Tom B.

"That's right. And don't forget, Tom B.," Willie went on, "this is a funeral, not a party. The man who passed away wanted a band to play hymns and dirges on the way to the graveyard. It's our way of honoring a friend. Wait outside the church and watch. And be respectful, boy."

"Yes, sir."

Willie joined the other musicians near the door of the church. They talked quietly, waiting for the funeral service to end. A few minutes later a black funeral coach and three black limousines lined up at the curb. A solemn man dressed in black except for white gloves got out of the funeral car and walked over to Willie. They talked quietly together. At a nod from Willie, the band lined up in front of the funeral car. The church door opened. The men in the crowd took off their hats and stood in respectful silence as the casket was gently carried from the church by six pallbearers. When the casket was placed in the funeral car, relatives and friends of the deceased, many of them weeping, got into the limousines.

Willie nodded to the man who played the kettle drum. Muffled with a black cloth thrown over it, the drum rattled softly, and the bass drum boomed three times. The band played "Nearer, My God, to Thee," in notes slow and solemn. As they played, the men walked slowly up the street followed by the funeral car, the limousines, and other automobiles.

It was a solemn procession. As the funeral car passed, people bowed their heads. One man said, "Good-by, George," to the flower-draped casket in the slow-rolling automobile. The crowd moved with the procession, keeping as close to the band as possible. The band played "Just a Closer Walk with Thee." A lady on the sidewalk with a child in her arms sang, unmindful of the people around her.

> "When this feeble life is o'er,
> Time for me will be no more.
> Lead me safely to Thy shore,
> To Thy kingdom's shore, to Thy shore."

Tom B. walked beside Willie. He felt like crying. When the wail of the saxophone led the "West Lawn Dirge," tears came to Tom B.'s eyes. He wiped them away with the back of his hand and looked to see if anyone was watching.

The musicians marched to the cemetery fourteen blocks away. When people stood beside the open grave, the band played "The Old Rugged Cross." In a few minutes it was over.

The crowd drifted toward the street at the entrance of the cemetery. The members of the band strolled to the street one by one and formed a line. The crowd was tense with excitement. The drums were no longer muffled. The "boom boom" of the bass was rich and full-throated. The band broke into "When the Saints Come Marching In." This was not the solemn measure of the hymn. It was jazz, joyful jazz. The crowd roared. In one second a hundred men, women, and children were dancing and marching in the streets.

Tom B. looked at Willie and shook his head, stunned. Willie grinned and waved his hand. The street was soon packed with people coming out of their houses to join the parade. Sadness was forgotten in this happy flow of emotions. Everyone was laughing, shouting, hand-clapping, and dancing to the music.

Someone touched his arm. Tom B. jumped with fright. It was Allan.

"Hi, Tom B.," Allan said.

Tom backed away out of reach. He looked warily at Allan and didn't answer.

"Did you find the funeral interesting?" asked Allan. Worry showed in his eyes.

Tom B. could not reply. Allan came to the point.

"Your grandmother is very worried about you, Tom B. Come on. I'll take you home on my motor scooter."

"Don't want to ride on no motor scooter. Don't want to go home. She took my trumpet mouthpiece."

Allan walked toward Tom B. speaking softly. "Tom B., you must go home. The police are looking for you."

Tom B. backed away faster. Allan made a dash for him, but he ducked under Allan's outstretched arm and ran through the crowd. He dodged into a swirl of moving people. When he saw that he had lost Allan, he stopped running. He had gotten away!

What makes him think he can run as fast as me? Tom B. asked himself.

He was angry too. Now I'll miss the end of the parade. It looks like everybody's trying to keep me from music.

He took a bus headed for Canal Street. As he got farther from the parade, he felt safer. I guess I can keep out of everybody's way, he boasted to himself.

Hopping off the bus, he walked over to Royal Street and bought two hot dogs and a large orange pop. As he counted out his change, he saw that he only had fifty-five cents left. "I better make me some money," he muttered, wishing he had his shoeshine box.

Wandering over to Chartres Street, he watched some trucks being unloaded. He walked up Chartres to Jackson Square. Sidewalk artists were busy, their work displayed on the iron fence that went around the small

park. Tourists stopped and watched while they painted or made drawings of New Orleans scenes.

Tom B. looked at some colored chalk drawings on the fence. The artist, in a half-serious voice said, "Want your picture done? Only four dollars."

"No, thank you," replied Tom B. "I don't have the money."

"I'll tell you what," the man said, "you have an interesting face. Sit down and I'll draw you for nothing, except the picture will be mine. O.K.?"

"O.K.,"answered Tom B. He sat in the chair. The artist worked fast. People gathered around the artist and watched as he sketched Tom's face. Tom B. felt very important.

Twenty minutes later the artist announced, "Finished." He hung the picture of Tom B. on the iron fence. Tom B. looked at it and nodded in approval.

"Looks just like me. Mom would like it."

A pang of loneliness shot through him. He quickly walked away and headed toward the nearby Bienville Street Docks.

10

The River

Tom B. wanted to go where he could be alone. He needed to think. The Bienville Street Dock Warehouse would be just the place, if he could just get past the guards and slip in through the big door. Longshoremen were loading lumber. Tom B. watched the huge loads sway back and forth and marveled at the crane operator. Pulling and pushing gears and cranks, he shifted the lumber from the dock to the dark hold of the ship.

"Boy," said a voice. Tom B. jumped with fright.

"Get out of here," the foreman told him. "Loading lumber is dangerous. You might get hurt."

Tom B. turned as if to go, but when the foreman was busy again with the lumber, Tom B. saw his chance. In a flash he ran through the open warehouse door and hid behind some boxes of sewing machines. Everything was still in the warehouse. There was only the noise of the crane as it lifted lumber from the dock.

He was tired. Slowly he made his way to the darkest part of the warehouse. Huge bales of cotton were stacked against the wall in the back. He climbed to the top of the pile and crawled back where the shadows lay deepest. As he rested he thought about his problems. His grandmother had sent the police after him. His friend Allan had tried to catch him, probably to turn him over to the police. Now he couldn't hear music at Preservation Hall or go to parades. He couldn't go home, and maybe even Willie would not teach him trumpet. Loneliness lay heavy on Tom B. He started to sob gently, but in a few minutes he rubbed his eyes fiercely and heaved a big sigh. Tired, he was so tired. He closed his eyes.

He dreamed that he was at a parade. Willie Lewis and his band were playing. A policeman walked through the crowd of people. Tom B. saw him and started to run. The policeman ran after him. Hands in the crowd reached out to stop him. They held him so that he could not run. Voices rumbled louder and louder. Tom B. awakened with a jump. There really were voices. He had heard one before, the foreman of the lumber gang.

"That's right, Officer," the foreman said, "he was wearing blue jeans and a blue-checkered shirt. I told him to get off the docks. Far as I know, he went."

"It's mighty kind of you to go through the warehouse. He could be in here, I suppose," said the police officer. Tom B. peered between two bales. He trembled with fear.

"There's a thousand places to hide in a place like this," the foreman said.

A couple of men came to the foreman. "We've checked the other end of the warehouse," said one, "and he's not there. I'll have the men spread out and see if the kid is hiding in this end of the building.

"Be sure to have a look around the cotton bales," the foreman directed.

Tom B. tensed. He knew that he would have to make a run for the door. Someone was coming toward him. He made himself as small as possible and waited, his heart beating wildly. He could hear the footsteps getting closer and closer. It was too much. He jumped up in front of the startled man, leaped off the bale of cotton, and ran frantically toward the open front door.

"Catch him! There he goes!" the man shouted. A man stationed at the door tried to stop him, but Tom B. easily slipped by him and ran out into the sunshine. As he raced along the edge of the dock he did not notice the coil of rope directly in his path. His foot hit the rope and he lost balance. For a sickening moment he swayed on the edge of the dock. Then with a yell of fright he plummeted into the deep water.

Tom B. tried to call for help, but the slimy river water got into his mouth. Coughing and spluttering, he thrashed the water as hard as he could. He did not know how to swim. His throat and chest hurt. Everything turned black. He did not hear the splash made by the police officer and the longshoreman as they dived into the water.

Tom B. woke up in a bed. The sun was high. He looked around and said, "It smells funny in here." He saw his grandmother standing beside his bed. "Hey, Mom."

She smiled. "Hey, Tom B."

He could see that she had been crying. "Where am I?"

"You're in Charity Hospital."

"How come?"

"You fell in the river. A policeman and longshoreman pulled you out. You had a close call, Tom B., a mighty close call." She put her handkerchief to her eyes.

Tom B. was upset. He looked at his grandmother and blurted out, "I missed you, Mom, and I was lonesome." Then the tears came streaming.

She took him in her arms. "Never you mind, Tom B., we're all right now, you and me. I suppose an old woman needs to learn more about boys."

He was still worried. "Am I all right with the police?"

"You're all right. I promised them you wouldn't run away any more. Was it O.K. for me to do that?"

"Sure was," he agreed, nodding his head. "No matter what, I'm staying home. It ain't no fun to sleep in the backseat of a car."

His grandmother laughed. "No, I suppose not. By the way, I had a phone call from a Mr. Clay Burke from the Jazz Museum. He read in the *Times Picayune* how you fell in the river."

"You mean I'm in the *Times Picayune*? Man, oh, man!"

"Sure you're in the paper. It's home for you to see." She went on. "Mr. Burke called to hope you get well. He said it was O.K. about the little accident in the Museum, and you're welcome to go there anytime. How about that?"

"Wow!" was all Tom B. could say.

"The nurse told me she wanted you to take a little nap before lunch."

"O.K., Mom," said Tom B., settling himself comfortably.

He was awakened by the rattle of food trays.

"Chow time," said the nurse's aid who carried in his tray.

"Look at this food—" said Tom B., "meat loaf, mashed potatoes, green beans, ice cream, and milk."

"Think you can eat it all?" the nurse's aide asked.

"I'm kinda hungry." He lost no time in finishing the food on the tray. His grandmother watched with a contented face.

There was a knock on the door.

"Come in," Tom B. said.

"Hey, Tom B.," said a familiar voice. Willie Lewis stood in the doorway.

"Mr. Lewis! Come on in."

Willie said, "I read in the *Times Picayune* that you were in the hospital, and I thought I'd pass by."

"I just finished my lunch," said Tom B.

"From the looks of your empty tray, your appetite is as good as it was at my house," chuckled Willie.

Then Tom B. remembered. "Mr. Lewis, this is my grandmother, Mrs. Williams. Mom, this is Mr. Lewis."

"I'm pleased to meet you, Mr. Lewis," said Mrs. Williams in a polite voice.

"Thank you. You've got a fine boy, Mrs. Williams."

"I know it," she answered. She seemed to grope for words as if it was hard for her to say what she had on her mind. She looked straight at Willie and said, "Mr. Lewis, I owe you an apology."

"What for?"

"For what I said about you."

Willie Lewis said nothing.

"But you're a deacon in your church and still you play jazz music. I—I don't understand."

"Maybe jazz music isn't as sinful as all that," Willie said gently. "It's people who are sinful, not music. I've been playing trumpet in my church since I was a boy. Sometimes I play hymns and on special occasions I play jazz there. The psalm says,

" 'With trumpets and the sound of the horn
make a joyful noise before the King, the LORD!' "

"I guess I never understood it that way," she said.

"But you sure understand boys, Mrs. Williams. You've done a fine job raising this one."

Mrs. Williams walked over to Tom B. and reached into her pocketbook. "I believe this is yours," she said, handing him the trumpet mouthpiece.

Tom B. whooped with joy. Then he grew serious.

"Will you please let Mr. Lewis give me lessons, Mom?"

"Indeed I will, if he doesn't charge too much," she said.

"Mrs. Williams, I got my lessons free from old-time jazz musicians and I want to do the same thing for the new generation. It's the way we keep the music alive. The old teach the young."

"I appreciate your offer," said Mrs. Williams proudly, "but if it's good, it's worth paying for. Tom B. saves his money. He can pay for his lessons and buy himself a trumpet."

"Very well," said Willie. "We'll talk about it and settle on a price."

"Very well," she replied.

Tom B. beamed at her. He could hardly believe what he'd heard.

"I expect," she went on, "Tom B., if you keep in mind that your most important job is school, why maybe there will be time to go to Preservation Hall once in a while."

Her eyes twinkled.

Willie Lewis came over to the bed. "Young man, I'll expect you next Saturday for your first lesson. I can loan you my old trumpet till you get enough money together to buy one."

It was all happening too fast for Tom B. He could hardly tell whether this was one of his dreams or whether it was real.

"Just one thing," went on Willie Lewis. "I don't teach trumpet to any boys that sleep in cars or hang around docks."

"Oh, no, sir!" Tom B. looked sideways at his grandmother. "I just don't think they's going to be any more teachers meetings. And cars sure ain't comfortable for sleeping. And I done seen all they is to see down on the docks." The feel of slimy, choking water swept over him again, and he shuddered against the pillow. But he squeezed the cool, smooth trumpet mouthpiece, and the terrible feeling went away.

"Good," said Willie. "I'd better go now. The missus gave me some errands to do. All right, Tom B.?"

"All right, Mr. Lewis!"

When he had gone, Mrs. Williams reached into her pocketbook. She brought out the big oatmeal spoon and waved it threateningly. "When you get home," she said. "I don't want you to laze around in bed mornings, or I'll crack you with my spoon."

Tom B. laughed and reached for his grandmother. Her arms went around him tight, and joy sang through him.

Biography of Jerome Cushman

Jerome Cushman was graduated from Park College, Parkville, Missouri, and received a B.S. in Library Science from Louisiana State University. He became interested in children's books when he was librarian of the Salina, Kansas, Public Library and his interest grew as he told stories to his three children.

He began his career as a chief librarian by telling stories to every child in the public and parochial school system, up to grade seven. At the end of fourteen years he was telling stories to over four thousand boys and girls. He recruited local community theater adults to present puppet shows for boys and girls, writing and adapting scripts from folktales.

Mr. Cushman is active in state, regional, and national library affairs and has served as president of the Kansas Library Association and of the Mountain-Plains Library Association. He has also served as a member of the Council and Executive Board of the American Library Association.

In 1965 he became Lecturer in Children's Literature

for the School of Library Service and the Department
of English at UCLA, where he reaches one thousand
students each year with children's literature.

A widower, he remarried in 1969. A small boy has
has been added to the family, so he is starting the story-
telling trek once more.